A Zed & Two Noughts

A Zed & Two Noughts

PETER GREENAWAY

faber and faber

LONDON · BOSTON

First published in 1986
by Faber and Faber Limited
3 Queen Square London WC1N 3AU

Photoset and printed in Great Britain by
Redwood Burn Ltd, Trowbridge, Wiltshire

British Library Cataloguing in Publication Data

Greenaway, Peter
A Zed & Two Noughts.
I. Title
822'.914   PR6057.R3/

ISBN 0–571–13767–9

'. . . you are the last and we are already finished'.

Author's Note

The text printed here is the full script of *A Zed & Two Noughts* that was used as the master-copy when shooting the film in Holland in the spring of 1985. It is therefore fuller than the text of the film completed in the autumn of 1985. Most of the material existing here and absent in the film is dialogue – some two hundred or so lines scattered throughout the eighty scenes which, in the necessary shaping and pruning of the film-editing process, were found to be surplus to the requirement of a narrative that could be seen directly on the screen rather than visualized off the page. A perfectionist reader checking script with finished film will also find some minor re-arrangement of scenes.

It seems to me that the comprehension and enjoyment of the reader, as opposed to the viewer, is best served in printing this version rather than a slavish definitive transcription. Besides, what film is truly definitive? By the time you see the film it may very well be sub-titled, re-edited, shortened, even censored, and every film is viewed at the discretion of the projectionist, the cinema manager, the architect of the cinema, the comfort of your seat and the attention of your neighbour.

A Zed & Two Noughts received its world première at the London Film Festival on 30 November 1985 and subsequently opened at the Lumière cinema, London, on 5 December, 1985.

Cast:

ALBA BEWICK	Andrea Ferreol
OSWALD DEUCE	Brian Deacon
OLIVER DEUCE	Eric Deacon
VENUS DE MILO	Frances Barber
VAN HOYTEN	Joss Ackland
VAN MEEGEREN	Gerard Thoolen
CATARINA BOLNES	Guusje van Tilborgh
JOSHUA PLATE	Jim Davidson
FELIPE ARC-EN-CIEL	Wolf Kahler
FALLAST	Geoffrey Palmer
STEPHEN PIPE	Ken Campbell
BETA BEWICK	Agnes Brulet

Crew:

Director of Photography	Sacha Vierny
Story Editor	Walter Donohue
Music	Michael Nyman
Film Editor	John Wilson
Producers	Kees Kasander
	Peter Sainsbury
Writer and Director	Peter Greenaway

I would like here to acknowledge all those many people who have contributed to the making of the film of *A Zed & Two Noughts*. There is no question whatsoever that it could have been made for money alone; the long hours worked, the care for detail, the enthusiasm of all concerned, are proof of that. Thank you.

Peter Greenaway

Introduction

The film begins with a car crash. Outside a zoo, a Mute Swan smashed into the windscreen of a white Ford Mercury, registration number NID 26 B/W, driven by a woman wearing white feathers called Alba Bewick. An accident?

'Five thousand accidents happen every day – bizarre, tragic, farcical. They are Acts of God, fit only to amaze the survivors and irritate the Insurance Company.'
'This one is different for God's sake.' Or Darwin's.

Although there were many visual sources for the origin of *A Zed & Two Noughts*, the three most conveniently recognizable ones can be accredited to a tape, an ape and a borrowed photograph.

The tape was a three-minute time-lapse film of the decay of a common mouse first shown on a BBC Horizon programme in 1981. Thanks to the speeding up of the time-lapse material, it was seen that maggots acted in unison on a corpse, devouring it systematically in a pack. It was the camera-operator's ambitious hope one day to film the decay of an elephant.

The ape lived in Rotterdam Zoo and had only one leg. The animal had been chained in a backyard. The chain had bitten into the leg and the spread of infection was only to be prevented by amputation. When the animal climbed and swung about in its cage there were times when it seemed that the missing leg was no impediment at all. Its incapacity had, it seemed, been victoriously overcome.

And the photograph had been a generous loan to me in 1978 for use in an encyclopaedic film called *The Falls*. It showed a confidently smiling woman standing between the elegant, enigmatic, identically-twinned Quai Brothers, puppeteers and filmmakers whose methods of film-animation were not so very different from the concepts of squeezing time that had made it possible to see how the maggots had devoured the mouse carcase.

With various degrees of conscious and subconscious manipulation, these three primary visual sources were welded into a script that, since all the best things come in threes, permitted a close view of the trauma of loss and the fascination of decay; it offered a platform for consideration, without judgement, of man's persistently dubious relationship with animals and provided another opportunity to play with taxonomies – used, no longer used, wholly invented, unlikely, irrelevant or impossible – Darwin's Eight Evolutionary Stages of Natural Selection, the seven days of Genesis, the Greek Pantheon, the twenty-six letters of the alphabet, the diminishing number of authenticated Vermeer paintings . . . and so on.

The overall visual master-of-ceremonies of the film was to be Vermeer – adroit and prophetic manipulator of the two essentials of cinema – the split-second of action, and drama revealed by light. It cannot be proved that Vermeer's 'Milkmaid' is a painting representing one twenty-fourth of a second of seventeenth-century time, exposed at f8, but the direction of the light is certain: always from the left of frame, coming from a source four and a half feet off the ground. The intention to preserve this discipline rigorously in *A Zed & Two Noughts* was, as often as not, eroded by the vagaries of the locations and the free-range habits of animals, but the spirit was preserved.

Homage to Vermeer in composition, gestures and picture detail is frequent and unabashed. Vermeer's wife, Caterina Bolnes, is there, manifest as 'The Lady in the Red Hat', as is Vermeer's prime faker, Van Meegeren, the man who successfully convinced Europe (and Goebbels) that there were certainly more than twenty-six authenticated Vermeers in existence.

To match the content, the major compositional device is twinship and symmetry. The facts, fictions, mythology and apocrypha on twins is limitlessly rich – two of everything, the search for your other half, mistaken identities, mirror-imaging, substitution, the *doppelgänger*, the lateral line and cloning. Plots, plays, scripts and libretti are certainly not infrequent on the subject. The archetypal pair of twins, Castor and Pollux, the astrological Gemini, born out of an egg from the union of a swan and a god provide *A Zed & Two Noughts* with its central pivot, the brothers Oliver and Oswald Deuce, the two letter Os, the two noughts, the two zeros of the film's title – put together to make a spectacle of themselves.

And the brothers work in a zoo. It could be said now that all animals live in zoos, whether it is a zoo in Regent's Park, London or a Nigerian Game Reserve. Perhaps what's left to argue is only the zoo's quality. Thanks to the Voyage of the Beagle, the demise of the work-horse, the plans now being made to leave Earth and our present dubious passion with ecology, our relationship with animals has changed dramatically in the last hundred years; but has our sense of responsibility improved? And have we acknowledged another responsibility? What about mermaids, centaurs, the Sphinx, the Minotaur, werewolves, vampires, and that proliferating zoo of contemporary hybrids. If one parent was an animal now familiar behind bars at the zoo, who was the other?

Are animals like car-crashes – Acts of God or mere Accidents – bizarre, tragic, farcical, plotted nowadays into a scenario by an ingenious storyteller, Mr C. Darwin? Is classical Venus the biblical Eve? If the evolutionary span of life on Earth is represented by a year of 365 days, and man made his appearance at eight o'clock on 31 December, did woman arrive just after eight? Was Adam a twin, and if so, what happened to his brother? Is a zebra a white horse with black stripes, or a black horse with white stripes?

Cinema is far too rich and capable a medium to be merely left to the storytellers.

1. PROLOGUE: THE ZOO GATES (*title sequence*)

The letters Z, O and O dominate the front entrance gates of a capital city zoo. They are made of glass and they tower up two giraffes high. They are the width of one elephant and the colour of bottled blue ink. The two Os just touch one another, the Z is a little apart. They dwarf their surroundings.

Standing at the front gates is a solitary zoo functionary, a zoo guide/zoo messenger, in a white and blue uniform with a noticeable number of silver facings on his jacket. He is young – in his middle twenties, fair-haired with a 'bright' face. His name is JOSHUA PLATE. *He watches absentmindedly as a boy and a girl, both aged around ten, struggle to drag a very prominently marked, black and white Dalmatian dog into the zoo. The dog resists, barking and whining.*

It is late afternoon in spring. The sky seen through the upper parts of the giant blue letters is beginning to glow pink and orange – the same colour – almost – as flamingoes. The pavements are wet and slippery, just right for disabilitating accidents.

The title of the film, A Zed & Two Noughts, *is superimposed across the wet pavements.*

Loud, strongly rhythmic music dominates the sound track.

2. PROLOGUE: THE TIGER

A tiger paces in a dirty cage. The cage is cramped. No more than three tiger-lengths across, perhaps four tiger-lengths wide. On the grey concrete floor, washed with tiger urine, decorated with dark piles of ordure, are the stale remains of the tiger's last meal, a savaged zebra's head identified by its large eye-sockets and its striped face and its yellow incisors.

The relentless pacing of the tiger in its cramped cage has worn away the paint layers at the back wall of the cage: the top surface of turquoise, the undercoat of white, and the successive layers of colouring down to the pink plaster and the red friable brick.

In front of the tiger's cage, and on our side of the bars, a man sits on a folding chair. He is hunched in concentration. He is casually, even scruffily dressed. His name is OLIVER.

He is an animal behaviourist on permanent staff at the zoo, and he watches the tiger closely, counting the number of lengths it paces, keeping a tally by using a counter whose trigger he presses down with his right-hand thumb every time the tiger turns. Already the tiger-counter shows the number of 676, the square of 26.

The rhythmic musical accompaniment of the previous shot continues and emphasizes the monotonous pacing of the animal. After some sixty seconds it is imperceptibly joined by the sound effects of a car travelling quite fast. The acoustics of the music change to evoke a car radio – somewhat tinny, filtered, and higher in register. There is a rapid succession of ambivalent noises that evoke the beating of large wings, the sound of a smashing of windscreen glass, a very pronounced skidding, unmistakable screams and a pronounced crash.

3. PROLOGUE: THE CRASH I

A car – a large, white Ford Mercury registration number NID 26 B/W, has just crashed on a busy road near the centre of a capital city. It lies shattered. Beyond it across the busy road is a hoarding carrying a large poster that features a tiger.

Wedged into the shattered windscreen is the large, bloodied body of a swan. Feathers and glass-shards litter the car's bonnet. Pinned into the front driving-seat of the crumpled car is a woman screaming with pain. Her name is Alba Bewick. She has a mane of red hair. In the back seat are two other women. They sit upright, very close together, their shoulders touching and their heads almost touching. They are very smartly dressed, good-looking, aged in their late twenties. One wears a feathered hat. Physically, they appear to be unmarked by the crash, but both are dead. One has her eyes open and her mouth closed, the other has her eyes closed and her mouth open.

Against the dull roar of the city, the woman screams and the car radio continues to play the music it played over the previous shot – 'the tiger-music' – shrill, tinny and relentless. The tiger on the poster appears to hover over the crashed car.

18

4. PROLOGUE: THE GORILLA

The screams of the woman trapped in the car become the threatening, aggressive screams of a female gorilla in a glass-fronted cage in the ape house at the zoo.

The gorilla has only one leg. Her disability is not so crippling as could be imagined, so invaluable and strong are her long arms. The animal has been crippled for a long time.

The cage/compound is yellow-tiled, with wood and metal swinging apparatus and four large black tyres suspended on chains.

On the other side of the cage is a glass-fronted door into the connecting corridor used by the animals' keepers for feeding and cleaning out. A man sits behind this door with a large stills-camera on a tripod. His name is OSWALD. *He is smartly dressed in a suit, tie and polished shoes; he is clean-shaven and his hair is carefully combed. He is taking photographs of the gorilla – observing its movements. Every ten seconds or so he takes rapid bursts of photos; the staccato clicking of the camera shutter can be heard above the noise of the animals – the enclosed space of the ape house giving all sounds a boomy resonance. The camera clicks are accompanied with synchronous flash-lights. Around him on the floor are numerous pieces of camera equipment.*

The photos he is taking will record the animal's movement in a collection of Muybridge-like stills which will be seen later in the film.

5. PROLOGUE: THE CRASH 2 *(ending in credits sequence)*

The large body of the swan wedged in the shattered glass of the car windscreen fills the film frame. Its head is bent back on itself in a parody of its orthodox gracefulness.

Two policemen in the foreground – one dips his finger into egg yolk that is spattered on the bonnet – the heat of the engine has 'poached' it. He brings his finger to his mouth and tastes the egg without comment. The other is going through the contents of ALBA BEWICK's *handbag. It is full of a great number of keys and a large coloured photograph of a beautiful wild garden.*

The camera travels forward and through the shattered glass of the

windscreen so that the centre of attention becomes the driver – ALBA
BEWICK *– the woman with the flaming red hair. She has been
drugged unconscious. A bright red oxygen mask covers most of her
face and a blood-drip is strapped to her arm. Her red hair is damp
with sweat and blood. Her back is now supported by crisp white
pillows. Bright blue acetylene cutters are cutting her free from the
wreckage.*

*The roar of distant traffic and the sound of a passing passenger
jet, along with the other particularized noises, intermittently mask,
obscure and distort a radio conversation where only one party is
heard – ostensibly the voice of a traffic officer back at base.*

RADIO VOICE: ... a swan? ... what sort of swan? ... Leda?
... who's Leda? ... is she the injured woman? ... by
whom? ... laid by whom? (*Incredulously*) ... by Jupiter?
... who's he? ... was that the cause of death? ... a
female swan ... how do you know it was female? ... eggs?
... egg-bound ... was it wild? ... perhaps it was a wild
goose? ... mute? ... how do you know if it was mute if it
was dead? ... were its wings clipped? ... did it come from
the zoo? ...

*This conversation, distorted by radio interference and irregularly
masked by all the other noises present, persists throughout the shot.*

*Whilst this macabre scene is dispassionately viewed by the camera,
the peripheries of the image are alive with the orthodox car-crash
aftermath. There are three different artificial light sources
illuminating the crashed car in the late evening light – a harsh
orange ambulance flash-light, the red light of a police car and the
blue light of the acetylene cutters. Mechanics and ambulance staff
work on the crash. A press photographer is taking press photos.*

*The camera travels on until the centre of attention is now the two
dead women in the back seat of the car. They sit perfectly upright,
side by side; they are dead but they look as though they could be
asleep. This 'live' shot of the two women freezes into a grainy
newspaper photo which is held 'frozen' as a background to the credits
of the film which roll up.*

6. PROLOGUE: THE CRASH 3

OLIVER, *the animal behaviourist who works in the zoo, the man who was observing the pacing tiger in its cage, is at the site of the crash. He is readily identifiable by his hair and his clothes. The car has been towed away – the marks of the crash are still on the site – an unusual amount of glass-fragments, tyre skidmarks.*

It is night. The tiger poster is artificially lit from below, emphasizing the wrinkles in the paper, throwing extra light on the tiger's head.

OLIVER *stands at the side of the road – his gaze vacant. He looks up and down the road. He shuffles the glass-fragments with his foot. He bends down and examines the glass-pieces. Some of them are bloodied, sticky with attached swansdown. – There are several pieces of white and blue china. He kneels and begins to fill his pockets with the fragments. He does the job scrupulously, as though he were picking up diamonds. The odd bloodied swansdown feather goes into his pocket as well.*

7. PROLOGUE: HOSPITAL SURGERY

Through a set of medical appliances that suggest the confining bars of a cage, ALBA BEWICK *lies on the operating table in a hospital theatre. She is having her right leg amputated. It has been irreparably damaged in the car crash. She stares unseeing at the ceiling with open eyes, her hair combed out on a green pillow. The predominant colour is green – lights, gowns, drapes, tubes, gloves: green with touches of blood.*

The surgeon is tall. His name is VAN MEEGEREN. *He fingers down his mask to look at* ALBA BEWICK. *He wipes his face, bends down, moves a drape to partly expose* ALBA BEWICK'*s breasts, and kisses her cleavage. He resumes his work. The instruments of surgery lie neatly in a row. He is watched all the time by a woman in a large red hat –* CATERINA BOLNES.

8. PROLOGUE: THE FIGHTING SWANS

The film frame is filled with a great scurry and rumpus of white wings and feathers. For a moment the significance is ambiguous. Only the violence is apparent. OSWALD, *the photographer, is fighting with swans.*

On the site of an ornamental pond near a swan's nest, in the suburbs of the capital city, OSWALD, *in confused reparation for a loss yet unexplained, battles vehemently with two female swans. His nose is bloodied, his shirt sleeves are in shreds, he is exhausted, panting, struggling on his back on the wet flagstones, under the drifting spray of an ornamental fountain. His trousers are torn. They have slipped from his waist in the struggle. He is losing them about his thighs. His face is smeared with blood and mud.*

The swans make off, hissing, and beating their wings. OSWALD *is left dazed and bleeding, a smashed swan's egg down his shirt front and trousers. Battered eggshells are crumpled in the crux of his legs. There is a suggestion of sexual assault. He nurses a bruised arm, and he is soaked. Exhausted, he continues to hurl abuse at the departing swans.*

9. PROLOGUE: OLIVER MOURNS (IN THE BATHROOM)

OLIVER *sits naked in his bath. The bathroom is dramatically and extravagantly lit with a desk lamp that has been placed on a white tiled floor. The lamp floods the floor with light and throws the walls into almost unrelieved darkness. The water in the bath is a clear green and throws reflections of ripples on to the ceiling.*

OLIVER *is awkwardly hunched up, his head in the crook of his right arm, his knees pulled up. He looks in pain. He has a pair of earphones clamped to his ears. From the loud tinny noise that can be heard, he evidently has the music turned up very loud. It is not possible to decipher what the music is. He sucks his thumb, and through it wails and sings along with the tune in his earphones. The sound he makes emerges as a painful, tuneless wail, the melody indecipherable. He sounds like a demented wounded animal. There is no relievable humour in his situation.*

Covering a large area of the bathroom floor are stacked newspapers – mint new, carefully folded – all of them open at a large news item covering the car crash. Prominent on the page is the large photograph of the crash showing the two dead women seated in the back of the car. OLIVER *has placed on several of the photographs glass-shards from the crash – they shine like diamonds in the light. Some of the shards are still accompanied by damp, bloodied feathers.*

10. PROLOGUE: OSWALD MOURNS

In the zoo laboratory OSWALD *sits hunched over a table at the far
side of a large room – beyond a collection of a dozen or so cameras
set up to time-lapse record the growth of various animal and
vegetable specimens. The cameras are all set at different time
intervals and expose their pictures with the flick of a flash-light –
some at five seconds, some at ten, fifteen, twenty, thirty seconds.
There are other permanent light sources – a blueish heat-lamp over a
tray of seedlings, a red developing light over an aquarium of water-
weed.*

*The camera travels slowly across this room of whirring, flashing
equipment towards the figure of* OSWALD. *He sits over a light-box
laid horizontal on the table, the light reflecting up at his tear-stained
face. On the light-box are six coloured 4 × 4 transparencies of the
one-legged gorilla that we saw* OSWALD *filming previously. The
gorilla looks awkward and very lame.*

OSWALD *has his fingers plunged deep in his hair, the hair wound
painfully tight around his fingers, obviously pulling at his scalp. The
inanimate cameras whirr and click around him – cameras recording
the slow growth of plants, the opening of blossoms – whilst* OSWALD
mourns the death of his wife.

11. PROLOGUE: THE BURIAL

*A marble mausoleum with monuments of naked children and docile
animals inside a brightly lit church interior.* OLIVER *and* OSWALD
*sit on a long low marble bench. For the first time they are seen
together. They sit in exactly the same relationship as their dead wives
did in the crashed car – upright and still. They both have bunches of
flowers on their laps – each bunch is different.* OSWALD's *bunch is
discreet, neat and wrapped primly in cellophane;* OLIVER's *bunch is
untidy, poorly wrapped, the brightly coloured flowers large and
overblown.*

*Though the two men are dressed differently and hold themselves
differently, one makes a small gesture that momentarily makes him
look a little like the other one. The casual observer might
momentarily think that the two men are related. Both men sit
stunned with grief at the sudden death of their wives. They speak
quietly and never once look at one another.*

23

OSWALD: My wife was five feet, seven inches . . . and she weighed 126 pounds – pound for pound . . . how fast does a woman decompose?

OLIVER: Six months . . . maybe a year. Depends on the conditions.

(*There is a long pause.*)

OSWALD: Does being pregnant make any difference?

OLIVER: No.

OSWALD: And the baby?

OLIVER: How far gone was she?

OSWALD: Perhaps ten weeks.

OLIVER: Then you'd never know.

(*Another pause.*)

OSWALD: (*Speaks very quietly as though to himself, then stares at the floor*) I cannot stand the idea of her rotting away.

(*Long pause, as* OLIVER *pulls a small snail off his bunch of flowers.*)

What is the first thing that happens?

OLIVER: The first thing that happens is bacteria set to work in the intestine.

OSWALD: What sort of bacteria?

OLIVER: *Bisocosis populi*. There are supposed to be one hundred and thirty thousand *bisocosis* in one lick of a human tongue . . . (*Pause*) . . . two hundred and fifty thousand in a French kiss. (*Said lugubriously.*) First exchanged at the very beginning of creation when Adam kissed Eve.

OSWALD: Suppose Eve kissed Adam?

OLIVER: Unlikely . . . she used her first one hundred thousand on the apple.

(*Both men stare absent-mindedly. There is a long pause before the scene is cut.*)

12. PROLOGUE: THE CRASH (LAYING FLOWERS) 4

The two men are at the scene of the car crash. The advertisement poster featuring the tiger is being replaced – it is being pasted out with large sheets of white paper by workmen with ladders.

OLIVER *and* OSWALD *stand where the bonnet of the car was – they look about them. They are still in the clothes they wore to the*

*funeral. They throw down flowers from their bunches and the
blossoms get crushed by the passing cars. A policeman approaches
them. There is a conversation that we cannot hear. Eventually and
without much protest, they place the remainder of their flower-
bunches on the kerbside and they make to leave. The slipstream of
the passing cars scatters the flowers.*

*The advertisement poster is now obliterated with white paper, save
for the tiger's head. As we watch, the last sheet is pasted over the
tiger's head – the tiger image is now obliterated and the screen is
white – ripe for a new beginning. The Prologue is over.*

13. 'CREATION' FOR OLIVER
*On to the blank white sheets of the obliterated poster is cut a
dramatic and beautiful image – an image of creation that is now
familiar from a hundred natural history films – the sort of shot whose
intention is to conjure up the Beginnings of Life on Earth. A piece of
film, no doubt shot alongside a hot-water geyser in Iceland – a mud
pool of hissing, steaming, bubbling water with a fringe of salt-
incrusted algae – accompanied with a commentary read in a dutifully
awed voice claiming the dispassionate voice of science.*

COMMENTARY: . . . and life almost certainly started at such a
conjunction in the primaeval seas – of shallow water, sunlight,
warm salts and electric storms.

A medium wide shot of OLIVER *in a comfortable chair of a viewing
theatre cum lecture hall. He stares at the screen, the screen
illuminating his face. He is unshaven and untidy, his eyes puffy. He
takes neat gulps from a small glass of whisky.*

14. FIRST HOSPITAL VISIT TO ALBA BEWICK
It is late afternoon in the hospital ward where ALBA BEWICK *is
convalescing after her leg amputation.* ALBA BEWICK *lies on a very
white-sheeted bed, with her flaming red halo of hair spread out
across the pillow. There is a space in the bed where her right leg
should be. Her face is ashen. She stares at the ceiling, her mouth
firmly closed. On either side of the bed sit* OLIVER *and* OSWALD.

*They have brought flowers – similar to the ones they took to their
wives' funeral. There is a long pause. The two men stare at the
patient.*

OLIVER: How are you feeling?

ALBA: Short of a leg . . . in the land of the legless, the one-
legged woman is queen . . . (*Said with a self-mocking voice,
totally devoid of pathos.*) . . . there was a legless whore in
Marseilles during the war who was very wealthy . . . she
rarely left her bed because she couldn't . . . she'd had both
her legs amputated at the groin. Imagine that gentlemen.
No limbs to hinder entry. She was treated with great
affection and regard and had a great many lovers. She died
young. Some admirers thought she might like to be buried
in a short coffin . . . others thought that the empty space
should be filled with flowers. In the end, of course, her
family turned up – and they had the corpse fitted with
artificial legs. Imagine that. The body in all its delicious
detail fading away – leaving a skeleton with iron legs . . .
(*As an afterthought and briskly.*) . . . especially since the legs
had been made for a man called Felipe Arc-en-Ciel.

OSWALD: You've been very thorough in your research.

ALBA: I made it up. (*Said with a wry smile at their confusion.*) I
have now to find a Felipe Arc-en-Ciel to stop my crying –
and to discover what it is to have your legs borrowed by a
dead woman. (*She weeps.*)

(OSWALD *gets up and takes a brown paper bag from his pocket.
It's full of apples which he takes out and puts in a bowl beside*
ALBA's *bed. He looks at them and then takes one back, wipes
it with his hand and puts it in his pocket. There's a long pause.*)

OLIVER: How is your daughter?

ALBA: (*Briskly*) Beta is fine. She says my leg has walked off with
a Dutchman.

15. APPLE TIME-LAPSE
*In the back and harshly lit spaces of the time-lapse laboratory, where
up to a dozen experiments are being conducted at different camera
speeds,* OSWALD *sets up a time-lapse camera, fixing leads,
arranging focus. At a neighbouring workbench is* JOSHUA PLATE –

he watches OSWALD *out of the corner of his eye. He had arranged a group of crocodile eggs under a heat-lamp in front of a clicking time-lapse camera that takes a picture every ten seconds.* OLIVER *takes no notice of him – he stands hesitating in front of the camera equipment, then takes an apple out of his overcoat pocket – the same one he previously put there in* ALBA's *hospital ward. It's very green. He wipes it with a clean handkerchief and then places it on an experiment dish. He then takes it up again and self-consciously breathes on it, then licks it, and finally, after a quick look round the laboratory, he kisses it, and then takes a bite out of it. After this performance, he puts the apple back in the dish, the bite-mark turned towards the lens of the time-lapse camera. He stands a little, obviously relieved at having accomplished what he set out to do. He then looks through the view-finder of the time-lapse camera and arranges his shot. View through the camera view-finder – seeing what* OSWALD *sees – a green apple with a prominent bite out of it.*

16. NEAR THE ZEBRA ENCLOSURE
In the early morning, a woman walks among the animal cages wearing a tight skirt and black high-heeled shoes. She is dressed wholly in black, picked out with a minimum of white. She smokes a cigarette. She meticulously picks imaginary hairs off her black suit. The woman's name is VENUS DE MILO – *at least everyone calls her that. She wears a heart shaped brooch. The heart is one of the emblems of Venus. In the background a man – a cripple – is watching the animals. The cripple, of small significance in this shot, will gradually become more and more important and will eventually turn out to be* FELIPE ARC-EN-CIEL. VENUS DE MILO *meets* VAN HOYTEN, *Keeper of Owls. He is dressed in black, wears a black hat, and a Walt Disney Pluto badge on the lapel of his coat.*
VAN HOYTEN: (*Smiling*) Good morning, Milo. What are you
    doing?
MILO: Little enough.
    (*They both look towards the cripple.*)
VAN HOYTEN: You could come back with me.
MILO: Where?
VAN HOYTEN: Back of the owl cages.
MILO: There's no bed there.

27

VAN HOYTEN: Since when have you needed a bed, Milo?

MILO: Since my back ached – just now.

VAN HOYTEN: I'll give you £5 . . .

(*She shakes her head.*)

. . . and two pounds of calf's liver?

MILO: Do the owls go hungry for your pleasure?

VAN HOYTEN: . . . and not yours? Owls aren't that fussy, they'll eat a lizard. Would you rather have a lizard? . . . or a zebra afterbirth?

(MILO *turns away in contempt.*)

Tell me Milo, do you think a zebra is a white animal with black stripes, or a black animal with white stripes?

MILO: (*Ignoring the question*) Carry my shoes for me. (*She gives them to him and walks barefoot.*) There used to be a bed at the back of the vulture cages.

VAN HOYTEN: (*Laughing*) Come on Milo – then you were only fifteen – now you have less to bargain with.

MILO: (*Self-mockingly*) Now I have experience.

VAN HOYTEN: With animals? (*Laughing, and raising the price.*) All right – four pounds of calf's liver . . . and a drink? (*More sinisterly.*) Or we'll have to see about your license to practise.

MILO: (*Smiling and elaborately bargaining*) You only have to have a license to *start* a zoo, not to stock it – *you* could start a zoo, Hoyten, though you'd have to pay me to visit it . . . You can keep your free meat . . . I'll take £10 for half an hour . . . and the tail feathers of an American Bald Eagle?

VAN HOYTEN: (*Laughing*) Are you making a hat?

MILO: (*Smiling*) No – I'm writing a dirty story.

VAN HOYTEN: (*Confused*) We don't have an American Bald Eagle.

MILO: (*Looking hard at* VAN HOYTEN) I was forgetting – it's a black and white bird . . . then I'll settle for an introduction to Oliver Deuce.★

★*first mention of* OLIVER's *surname in the text.*

VAN HOYTEN: (*Laughing*) What do you want with him?

MILO: I could help him (VAN HOYTEN *laughs louder.*) . . . his wife's died . . . and I need a bath.

VAN HOYTEN: You can have a bath – provided I can watch.

MILO: Surprise, surprise (*She waves her arm embracingly across the cages of the zoo*) . . . that's what all we animals are here for, isn't it?
(*They leave the frame, leaving behind the cripple who is still totally absorbed in watching the zebra.*)

17. IN THE VIEWING THEATRE

OLIVER DEUCE *sits in the viewing theatre of the zoo laboratory. He stares at the screen – Part Two of the 'Life on Earth' series that relates and describes the growing sophistication of life in the early seas.* FALLAST, *the Zoo Controller and Keeper of Birds – a very authoritative figure in his late forties – enters the viewing theatre quietly.* FALLAST *watches the film silently for ten seconds before speaking. He wears a thunderbolt tie-pin: the Emblem of Jupiter.*

FALLAST: Oliver? I am sorry about your bad news. (*After a pause.*) Can the zoo help? (*After no answer and another pause.*) What are you watching?

OLIVER: (*Aggressively*) The beginnings of life.

FALLAST: (*After a pause*) Do you want to take time off?

OLIVER: (*Sharply*) No . . . it's cathartic.

FALLAST: What is?

OLIVER: Watching life begin.

FALLAST: Yes?

OLIVER: Yes – because I know how it ends.

FALLAST: How does it end?

OLIVER: With a swan.

FALLAST: (*Refusing to be surprised*) Yes?

OLIVER: . . . and a white car – a Ford Mercury – registration number NID 26 B/W, driven by a woman with flaming red hair, wearing white feathers – called Alba Bewick.

FALLAST: Then I'm sorry that you will find this film inaccurate.

OLIVER: (*Politely mocking*) Don't ruin it for me, Fallast . . . I'm going to take it in stages, it needs absorbing. I'm sure I must have got it wrong before, and I'm on the look-out for clues.

FALLAST: What sort of clues?

OLIVER: I need to separate the true clues from the red herrings.

FALLAST: I'm told that all eight parts of the second copy of this film are out on loan as well.

OLIVER: Are they? (*Said with great uninterest.*)

FALLAST: Yes ... and under the same surname as yours.

> (OLIVER *looks at* FALLAST – *their faces are illuminated by the screen.* OLIVER *shrugs and then looks back at the screen. There is a pause.*)

OLIVER: Perhaps someone else is also looking for red herrings.

18. 'CREATION' FOR OSWALD

OSWALD *is standing with his hands in his pockets, staring out into the dark evening. Behind him, in the room, is a large television set, which in black-and-white, is playing the same film we have just been viewing with* OLIVER DEUCE *in the zoo viewing room. Along the inside window-ledge is a collection of tigers – kitsch tigers, made of china, glass, plastic, metal, wood – ornaments and toys – anthropomorphic items – distorting and belittling the tiger.* OSWALD *is weeping and the television pours out its authoritative commentary.*

19. HOSPITAL VISIT

OLIVER's *first visit to* ALBA *in hosital on his own. He walks anxiously along the hospital ward to* ALBA's *bed, which is surrounded by screens – richly patterned with peacocks – the emblem of Juno. There is a gap in the screens which reveals a brightly sunlit interior. A glimpse of very white sheets, dazzling pillows and bright flowers and a naked back.* CATARINA BOLNES (*last seen at the operating theatre*) *leaves from behind the screen area, carrying an armful of brilliant red tulips.* OLIVER *hesitates, and* ALBA *speaks from behind the curtains.*

OLIVER: Madame Bewick? It's Oliver Deuce – Paula's husband.

ALBA: Oliver, what are you doing out there? Come in.

> (OLIVER *tentatively pulls at an opening in the screen curtain. He finds* ALBA *in bed, sitting up naked to the waist. She looks like a mature Juno by Titian. She is combing her long red hair, using a hand mirror propped up on her knee.* OLIVER *lets the curtain fall and he backs away.*)

OLIVER: I'll come back later.

ALBA: Oliver? Don't be shy. (*She laughs.*)

(ALBA *puts her arms into a dressing gown – a very white dressing gown with minimal black edging (the reverse of the clothing worn by Venus de Milo.*))

ALBA: Here, look, is this better? (OLIVER *hesitantly pulls back the screen curtaining.*) Don't apologise. What has a one-legged woman to hide? Sit here and talk to me.

(OLIVER *enters the screen tent around* ALBA's *bed – inside, it is even more inviting. The bright sunlight illuminates, shines and glints off chrome and china, whitening the white crisp sheets and illuminating a large vase of cut flowers. On the bedside table are three large coloured photographs of a lush overgrown garden.*)

ALBA: Where's Oswald?

OLIVER: He's . . . (*As off-hand as possible*) . . . just working. Work consoles him . . . I think.

ALBA: You think? . . . He's your brother,* isn't he?

first mention that the men are brothers

OLIVER: (*A little sheepishly*) Yes . . . I came alone to ask you . . . do you mind?

ALBA: No.

OLIVER: (*To settle his confidence,* OLIVER *picks up one of the coloured photographs from beside the bed*) Where's this?

ALBA: It's L'Escargot. I was born there.

OLIVER: It looks beautiful.

ALBA: It is. Is that what you wanted to ask me?

(OLIVER *takes a newspaper photo from his jacket pocket – the photo of the two wives in the back of the crashed car.* ALBA *looks at the photo – and there is a pause.*)

OLIVER: How did you first know my wife?

ALBA: I met her at the zoo . . . with my daughter . . . when I took Beta to the insect house to watch butterflies. Your wife said they ought to be let free. She didn't approve of zoos, did she?

OLIVER: No. Why is your daughter called Beta?

ALBA: (*Laughing at her explanation*) I wanted twenty-six children. Beta wasn't the first – the first one died. I had an infection – mercury poisoning – where I come from you take mercury to procure an abortion.

OLIVER: There aren't twenty-six letters in the Greek alphabet –
there's only twenty-three.
ALBA: (*With mocking politeness*) Thank you for your scholarship.

20. THE ZOO TIME-LAPSE LABORATORY
*In the zoo laboratory, the time-lapse cameras are photographing their
various experiments. In the foreground is* OSWALD DEUCE'S *camera
photographing the decaying apple – the apple is now covered in
mould.*

21. IN THE VIEWING THEATRE
OLIVER *is viewing a further episode of 'Life on Earth' –
crustaceans, slugs, snails. He is eating sandwiches in his lunch
break. There is a confused clattering at the door as someone tries to
get in. It's* JOSHUA PLATE. *He stumbles in, breaking* OLIVER'S
*concentration, letting a flood of sunlight slant across the dry, dusty
spaces of the viewing theatre.*
PLATE: Do you mind, Oliver – I heard you were in here.
        (*Looking at the screen.*)
OLIVER: (*Perfunctorily*) Sit down, Plate.
        (*There is a short pause; they both watch the screen.*)
PLATE: Funny smell in here.
OLIVER: It's me – I've stopped washing.
PLATE: I'm sorry about your wife.
OLIVER: (*Curtly*) So am I.
        (*There is a second pause.*)
PLATE: De Milo's been asking after you.
OLIVER: Everyone's pimp and messenger, eh Plate?
PLATE: Suit yourself.
        (*They watch the screen. Prawn-like crustaceans move across a
        sea-bed.*)

22. HOSPITAL VISIT
OSWALD DEUCE'S *first visit to* ALBA *on his own. He sits on her
bed.*
ALBA: I'm pleased you've come – where's your brother?
OSWALD: Oh – he's working – work consoles him.
ALBA: Are you sure?
OSWALD: No.

ALBA: Does it console you?

OSWALD: Yes – no. I'm trying to make it console me. I've nothing else now that Griselda's dead.

ALBA: Don't you have your brother?

OSWALD: (*Ignoring her*) I cannot understand why she's dead, so I'm going back to the beginning – to find out.

ALBA: To the beginning?

OSWALD: (*Holding his head in his hands*) I cannot stand the idea of her body rotting away . . . for nothing . . . or was it for some reason? (*To bridge the silence, he picks up the coloured photograph from beside the bed.*) Where's this?

ALBA: It's where I was born. It's called L'Escargot. I'd like to die there.

OSWALD: It looks beautiful.

ALBA: It is.

OSWALD: (*After a pause and still looking at the photograph*) Tell me what happened . . . in detail . . .

ALBA: You know what happened . . . Griselda and Paula were shopping for china.

OSWALD: What was Griselda wearing?

ALBA: A green coat . . . black shoes. We left there about three o'clock . . .

OSWALD: (*Interrupting*) Was she wearing a scarf?

ALBA: Yes. We turned out of the car park and . . .

OSWALD: (*Interrupting*) A pearl necklace and a wristwatch?

ALBA: Yes.

OSWALD: And a dark green dress with sequins at the throat?

ALBA: Yes – you know she was.

OSWALD: And . . .

ALBA: (*Interrupting*) Who's telling who?

OSWALD: (*Now off on his own reminiscences*) And black tights, white bra . . . and white knickers?

ALBA: If you say so.

OSWALD: And a scent called Blanche . . . and shaved underarms . . .

ALBA: (*Admonishingly*) Oswald.

OSWALD: . . . and an appendix scar . . . and very dark nipples . . . and . . .

33

(*There is a long, silent, sad pause.*)
Why was she buying china?

ALBA: She said she needed china. She bought four soup bowls and . . .

OSWALD: What were they like?

ALBA: They were white . . . with blue markings . . . and an egg-timer, and a milk jug . . .

OSWALD: An egg-timer. What the hell did she want with an egg-timer?

ALBA: (*Patiently*) I imagine, Oswald, to time eggs.

OSWALD: Why did she want to time eggs?

ALBA: Oswald, think what you're saying.

OSWALD: What else did she buy?

OSWALD: Paula wanted to go to the fishmonger. I bought a lobster.

OSWALD: What did you buy a lobster for?

ALBA: Oswald – this is getting silly.

OSWALD: Did my wife buy anything?

ALBA: Yes – prawns.

OSWALD: Prawns?

ALBA: Yes.

OSWALD: (*Getting up*) Thank you. I don't want to hear any more for the present.

ALBA: But all this is a long way back in the story.

OSWALD: Thank you for telling me. (*He makes to leave.*)

ALBA: Oswald – where are you going?

(OSWALD *hurries out of the ward,* ALBA *looking curiously after him.*)

23. BUTTERFLY HOUSE SEQUENCE

In a sunlit insect house, OLIVER DEUCE *is watching butterflies. Several butterflies are fluttering against a sunlit window in the glass panels above* OLIVER's *head.* OLIVER *opens the window to let the butterflies escape. Unbeknown to* OLIVER, JOSHUA PLATE *has been watching him.*

PLATE: Do you think that was wise?

OLIVER: (*Unabashed*) There were too many of them.

PLATE: Will they survive the cold?

34

OLIVER: This zoo is too crowded. There are too many staff for
a start – haven't you got anything better to do than
watch me?

24. BEDROOM PRAWNS
*Wearing the same clothes he wore at the hospital, OSWALD walks
into the bedroom he shared with his wife. It's untidy; the bed
dishevelled. Without taking off his belted raincoat, he puts down
several packages on the bed. He undoes the paper parcels, takes out
four white china bowls that have blue markings. He takes out an
egg-timer and a milk jug, and lays them out on the bed. He sits down
on a bedroom chair and stares at them. He then picks up the fourth
package and pours damp pink prawns into one of the bowls. He
bends his head, closes his eyes, and almost buries his nose in the bowl
of prawns. He takes a long breath and smells them deeply. He holds
the bowl close to his face, taking in the smell, and then he puts it on
the bed and begins to pace the room, still with his raincoat on. As he
walks back and forth – reminiscent of the pacing tiger at the zoo – he
brushes the wallpaper with his wet raincoat and makes marks on the
wall. All the time he eyes the china and prawns on the bed.*

25. THE NEWSPAPER CUTTINGS – MILO'S STORY
*In his bedroom at night, OLIVER sits naked, despondent. On the
bedside table and along a shelf by the bed, are several small
vivariums and several small laboratory specimen jars – all of them
contain snails. A woman sits on the side of the bed – it's VENUS DE
MILO. She is naked, her feet on the floor; close by her are her neatly
folded clothes. She is idly picking up newspaper cuttings from out of
the bed, reading them aloud and then putting them down to pick up
another one. OLIVER is arranging snails on a glass plate.*
MILO: (*Reading*) ... called Mute because, unlike the Bewick, it
is rarely heard ... eggbound ... there were no
children ...
OLIVER: Milo, have you ever done it with animals?
MILO: (*Unmoved, she briskly puts down the clippings*) If that's
what you want ... if it would help, I could invent for you.

35

It'll cost four pounds a story. That's what Anaïs Nin charged in 1927 – only she did it professionally. I haven't started professionally yet. Four pounds . . . or an introduction to a publisher, or a credit note to any large bookshop or . . .

OLIVER: (*Taking £4 out of his wallet on the bedside table*) All right . . . all right . . . go on . . .

MILO: Once upon a time, there were three bears . . .

OLIVER: No nursery stories.

MILO: Oh? . . . all right . . . A circus owner in Anchorage kept a polar bear called Fairbanks to entertain Eskimo wives . . .

OLIVER: Unlikely . . . and how come you know about Alaska?

MILO: I was attentive in geography . . . The bear had a narrow snout, a sweet nature and . . . a rough and probing tongue. It also liked honey.

OLIVER: It's beginning to sound like a bedtime story.

MILO: Isn't that just what you wanted?

OLIVER: . . . and there are no bees in Alaska.

(*He puts snails on the back of his hand. They begin to crawl on his body.*)

MILO: There are as many bees in Alaska as snails – why do you like snails?

OLIVER: They are a nice primitive form of life, they help the world decay . . . and they're hermaphrodite and can satisfy their own sexual needs.

MILO: I don't believe it.

OLIVER: Neither do I.

MILO: (*Returning to her story*) Given honey, this Alaskan bear was putty in your fingers. The circus owner, by leasing out the bear with a jar of honey, had two profitable sources of income . . .

OLIVER: This circus owner sounds like a friend of yours.

MILO: Polar bears, contrary to expectation, are not so enormously endowed as you would imagine . . .

OLIVER: Special knowledge?

MILO: (*Laughing*) No. Just observation . . . and the dissatisfied Eskimo wives at Port St George attacked the circus owner with the accusation that he was seriously overcharging . . .

OLIVER: (*Interrupting, irritated and a little sanctimonious*) God, Milo. This is another wingeing story about money and I disapprove of circuses . . .

MILO: I disapprove of zoos.

OLIVER: Shut up and get out.

MILO: But I haven't got to the erotic bits yet . . .

OLIVER: (*Red in the face with sudden anger*) Get out, get out.

(OLIVER *gets up in an irrational fury, snatches the newspaper clippings from* MILO's *hands, and pushes and drags her to the door of the apartment. His mouth is tightly closed, his face white.* MILO *struggles, abusing him and laughing at the same time, which infuriates* OLIVER *even more. He gets her to the door and pushes her out, naked, on to the outside landing. He slams the door and leans on it from the inside.*

Out on the landing, after a moment's hesitation, MILO *starts singing loudly 'If you go down to the woods today, you'd better go in disguise, for every bear that ever there was . . .'. She sings loudly to waken the neighbours.* OLIVER *hurriedly gathers up her clothes and throws them out on to the landing.*)

MILO: Be careful with those, you blockhead – it's best mohair. I spent a lot of time on that suit.

(OLIVER *slams the door shut and* MILO *shakes the suit out, folds it carefully over the suitcase banister rail, and then proceeds to dress carefully, still singing loudly, breaking up her singing with questions shouted through the apartment door.*)

MILO: What kind of stories does your brother Oswald like?

OLIVER: (*Through the door*) Why don't you go and ask him?

(*Inside the apartment,* OLIVER *puts his fingers in his ears. Still singing,* MILO *walks down the stairs – with the gestures of a striptease in reverse, putting her clothes on. Her voice echoes in the concrete stairwell. Inside the apartment,* OLIVER *is weeping. Through the door,* MILO *shouts.*)

MILO: And leave those little snails alone, you dirty old man.

(*An animal roars in the zoo.*)

26. THE ZOO LABORATORY
In the zoo laboratory with the dozen or so cameras time-lapse photographing various plant specimens – flower blooms and so on.

Three zoo employees are walking around the flicking and whirring cameras – they are all a little drunk. They are JOSHUA PLATE, *the zoo messenger,* VAN HOYTEN, *Keeper of Owls, and* STEPHEN PIPE, *Keeper of Fish.* PIPE *is in his late thirties – he wears green corduroy and is white-bearded. They come to where* OSWALD DEUCE *has set up his apple decay experiment.*

VAN HOYTEN: What's Oswald Deuce doing here?

PLATE: Watching an apple fade away.

VAN HOYTEN: How original. (*Sniffing*) What's that smell?

PIPE: (*Sniffing*) Dead fish.

> (*Following their noses, they move away to another flicking camera which is set up to record the decay of a plate of prawns. All three bend over the plate, dramatically holding their noses.* PIPE *looks at the identification and the job description note attached to the equipment.*)

PIPE: (*Reading*) Good Lord – it's Oswald Deuce again. What's he up to? (*Sniffing deeply.*) Prawns – what's the connection between apples and prawns? (*Giggling.*) What do gone-off prawns remind you of? What's the betting *all* of Oswald's wife smells like that now?

VAN HOYTEN: Maybe Oswald liked the smell so much he's trying to recapture it.

PLATE: You're disgusting.

VAN HOYTEN: And you're too prim for words . . . make him eat a prawn – Oswald won't mind.

> (VAN HOYTEN *and* PIPE *seize the struggling* PLATE *and taking a rotting prawn from the dish, they force it down* PLATE'*s throat.* PLATE *chokes and coughs.*)

27. IN OSWALD'S APARTMENT – MILO'S STORY
Seated in her underwear, MILO *is drinking tea at the kitchen table.* OSWALD *is fully dressed. A film screen and projector are set up in the bedroom.*

OSWALD: I hear you are supposed to tell animal stories.

MILO: That's right – five pounds – sixty for ten thousand words – one-eighth of what Pauline Reage got for the *Story of O*. I'm very reasonable. Or you can have it free if you can find me a publisher.

OSWALD: All right – take your clothes off and put this on. (*He gives* MILO *his wife's green coat – the one she was wearing at the crash.*) And this hat . . . open the coat down the front and fold your arms. (OSWALD *manoevres her into the position of his wife in the car crash.*) All right – start.

MILO: (*Totally unintimidated* MILO *does as* OSWALD *says and then starts her story*) In Botswana they keep a bull in a cave . . .

OSWALD: I've heard it.

MILO: You have? . . . (*She starts again.*) Well . . . in the 1870s in the Regent's Park Zoo in London . . .

OSWALD: (*Interrupting*) Wait a minute. (*He gets up and rearranges the feather in his wife's hat.*)

MILO: Am I allowed to go on?

OSWALD: Of course.

MILO: (*Starting her story again*) In the 1870s in the Regent's Park Zoo in London . . . there was an enclosure reserved for certain rare animals that came to be called The Obscene Animals Enclosure . . .?

(*She again waits to be interrupted, but* OSWALD *has walked away into his bedroom and is sitting on his bed watching and listening to her from a distance – the camera takes up his viewpoint as* MILO *continues with her story.*)

. . . One of the animals in this special enclosure was a toad – at least it had the body of a toad, but it also had certain other features that closely resembled – in shape – if not in size, parts of the anatomy that in Victorian England at that time – any time in fact – (*She is now totally engrossed in telling the story – a born story-teller*) . . . were normally kept hidden when a man was out walking . . . or indeed when he was eating . . . and drinking . . . and visiting the Regent's Park Zoo . . .

(*As the story continues,* OSWALD *gets up and begins to pace the bedroom – he rubs against the wallpaper in the same place as before – the wallpaper now shows considerable signs of wear.*)

28. THE HOSPITAL WARD – THE SPILT FLOWER WATER
OLIVER DEUCE *rushes into the ward and up to* ALBA's *bed.*
ALBA, *covered up to her shoulders with a thin sheet, is lying flat on*

her back. She is having her toenails manicured by a smartly dressed woman in a red hat – it is CATARINA BOLNES, VAN MEEGEREN's *assistant.*

OLIVER: It was all your bloody fault.

ALBA: What was?

OLIVER: The death of my wife.

ALBA: I see. Am I expected to take a pilot's licence? How could I anticipate swans?

OLIVER: You were travelling down Swan's Way, you were wearing feathers, and you were driving a Ford Mercury.

ALBA: So?

OLIVER: You were asking for trouble.

ALBA: Why?

OLIVER: You said you took mercury to procure an abortion. You were pregnant.

ALBA: For God's sake, how the hell did you know I was pregnant?
(CATARINA BOLNES, *despite her self-imposed demeanour of appearing uninterested in the conversation, is sufficiently amazed at this last turn in the conversation to stare at* ALBA.)

OLIVER: Pregnant women are notoriously unreliable – especially those trying to procure an abortion – it was all your fault – you bitch.
(OLIVER *throws fruit, including noticeably bright green apples, flowers and flower water over* ALBA *and the bed. The bed is drenched.* CATARINA BOLNES *calls for help. Nurses and orderlies rush in.*)

29. IN OSWALD'S APARTMENT – MILO'S STORY (CONTINUED)

In OSWALD's *apartment as before.* OSWALD *is pacing the bedroom, rubbing away at the wallpaper as he walks absentmindedly back and forth (like the tiger in the cage). Through the door into the living-room,* MILO *sits on a chair, dressed in the clothes that* OSWALD *gave her. She has finished her story.*

MILO: (*After a pause*) Was my story worth £10? . . . because I've got a dry throat.

OSWALD: Look at this.

(OSWALD *slumps down on his bed in the bedroom and flicks on a switch in the skirting board with his foot – the film projector comes to life and an image is projected on to a white screen. It's the time-lapse footage of the decaying apple from the zoo laboratory experiment. Through the door into the living-room,* MILO *takes off the hat* OSWALD *asked her to wear. She gets up and comes through.*)

MILO: Did I tell it well?

OSWALD: Yes. (*Absentmindedly*) Write it down and I'll see it gets published.

MILO: That's what your brother said.

OSWALD: (*Looking surprised*) Is it?

MILO: Isn't it time you two became a little more friendly?

OSWALD: (*Hesitating and a little guilty*) How is he?

MILO: He's miserable. Like you. (*She takes off the coat given her by* OSWALD *and begins to dress in her own clothes, watching the film on the screen all the while.*
Fourteen days of decay is condensed into one and a half minutes of film. Mould visibly creeps around the bite-mark, the green skin yellows – it goes brown – then emerald. The apple begins to collapse from within.)

OSWALD: Oliver says that the rot starts in the stomach.

MILO: With an apple?

OSWALD: (*Ignoring her*) . . . in the intestines . . . in the liver . . . the pancreas . . . the spleen . . . (*After a pause*) . . . near the womb. I cannot even imagine the idea of her rotting away. (*To leave* OSWALD *alone as he weeps,* MILO *goes into the living-room to finish dressing.*
The apple on the screen continues to decay. The skin blackens. The fruit noticeably dessicates. The film runs out of the projector revealing the bright light of the projector lamp glaring on the white screen.)

MILO: (*Off-screen voice*) I'm going to see Oliver – do you want me to give him a message?

OSWALD: (*Off-screen voice*) No. I've got nothing to say . . . Yes . . . tell him to look after himself.

30. OLIVER'S BATHROOM

In OLIVER's *brightly lit bathroom. On the tiled floor are piled neat stacks of newspapers and various packages of the glass fragments from the car crash, two bottles of red wine and a half-filled glass.* OLIVER DEUCE *sits on the bathroom floor, his back leaning against the bath. He is in the process of obsessively and meticulously swallowing glass fragments, taking them carefully from their screws of newspaper, putting them on his tongue and swallowing them with large gulps of wine. There is a trickle of blood on his lips and on his chin. There is blood on his palms, on his wrists and fingers. There is a ring on the apartment doorbell.* OLIVER *hears it but takes no notice. It rings and rings again as he – more hurriedly – chews on further glass fragments. Eventually* MILO *shouts through the letterbox – 'Oliver'.* MILO *peers through the letterbox, can see into the brightly lit bathroom and can see* OLIVER's *naked legs but no more. She shouts again – 'Oliver'. She takes a hairpin out of her bag and begins adroitly to pick the lock. Slow to get the door open, she calls through the letterbox.*

MILO: Oliver, what the hell are you doing?

OLIVER: (*Through a bloody mouth and swollen tongue*) Having breakfast.

> (MILO *manages to get the door open, strides into the bathroom, assesses the situation at once and kicks away the glass, the wine and the screws of newspaper.*)

MILO: Stop it, you bloody idiot.

> (OLIVER *replies by vomiting – vomit and blood. A piece of swans-down is attached to his lip with blood.*)

You pathetic idiot.

OLIVER: (*Pathetically*) It's only ice.

MILO: Ice floats – and you don't put ice in wine.

OLIVER: (*Sadly*) Since when has etiquette been your strong point. All right – phone for an ambulance. I've had enough.

MILO: (*Sarcastically*) Thank you. Shall I call Oswald?

OLIVER: No . . . all right, yes. Tell him – I'm bleeding. He'll come. He always used to come when I was bleeding.

31. HOSPITAL WARD

In the hospital ward by ALBA's *bed.* OLIVER *in a dressing gown sits*

on a chair beside the bed. He looks very white and haggard.
OSWALD *wearing a raincoat sits on the bed.* ALBA *makes a show of moving the glasses about the bedside table.*
OLIVER *smiles limply. There is a pause.*

ALBA: You were right – though I didn't deserve the soaking.

OSWALD: How was he right?

ALBA: I *was* pregnant. I not only lost a leg in that crash. I lost a child – though I was not by any means trying to.

OLIVER: (*With a faint smile*) Gamma is not a good name for a child.

ALBA: I have yet to work out my greater loss . . . but I know that I want another leg and another child – please.
(OLIVER *takes his hand from his dressing-gown pocket and reveals a small box. He opens the lid and takes from the box various pieces of china and glass which he lays on the bed.*)

OLIVER: As you can see, it was inferior china. The blue dye wasn't very fast. It comes off. (*He fingers the china pieces.*)

ALBA: (*Angrily*) What do you want to keep those for – throw them away, you stupid boy.
(OLIVER *picks up the pieces from the bed and drops them, one by one, into the wastebin beside the bed. There is a pause.*
OSWALD, *to bridge the gap in the conversation, picks up the photo from beside the bed and after looking at it a moment speaks.*)

OSWALD: I'd like to see this place.

ALBA: Then go and see – and come back and tell me how it's getting on. The key is in my bag. You could go together.
(*The two men look at each other.*)
So who found you?

OLIVER: De Milo.

ALBA: Who is she?

OSWALD: Her trade name is Venus, and her clients call her de Milo.

OLIVER: She knows more about animals than I do.

ALBA: Is she good – looking?
(*The brothers look significantly at each other.*)
It seems you both know her well.

OLIVER: She always dresses in black – all her clothes are black . . .

OSWALD: . . . when she wears them (*With the faintest of smiles.*)

ALBA: Oh?

OLIVER: She makes all her own clothes – she is a seamstress – (*With a smile.*) She is a beautiful stitcher.

ALBA: (*A little jealously*) Oh?

OSWALD: (*Trying to appease* ALBA) Venus de Milo is the zoo prostitute . . . When she's not watching the zebras, she waits for her clients at the Panda House . . . (*There is a pause.*)

ALBA: Oh? – and what's her speciality?

OLIVER: (*After another pause*) Bamboo?

(*They all laugh.* OLIVER *groans and holds his stomach and vomits.* OSWALD *gets up and helps him with a towel – in his anxiety he gets vomit over his fingers.* ALBA *looks on approvingly.*)

32. IN THE ZOO VIEWING ROOM

VAN HOYTEN *sits in the semi-darkness of the viewing theatre beside* JOSHUA PLATE, *his confidant. On the screen in front of them are beautiful images of coloured fish swimming in a sunlit ocean. After watching the images for a few moments – with the light from the screen moving on their faces,* VAN HOYTEN *speaks.*

VAN HOYTEN: What's Oliver looking for?

PLATE: I don't know – an answer to his wife's death?

VAN HOYTEN: He'll not find it here. This is just a straightforward account.

PLATE: Both brothers have taken out a copy . . .

VAN HOYTEN: Have I got to sit through them all? There's eight parts and this is only the second . . . and God – it's all such a dreary fiction.

(*Both men continue to watch exotic fish swim about near the ocean floor.*)

33. IN THE HOSPITAL WARD

In the hospital ward by ALBA's *bed.* OSWALD *has rigged up his projector and screen. The ward is in semi-darkness. The footage of the decaying prawns appears on the screen.* ALBA *is sitting up in bed with her arm around her daughter,* BETA. OLIVER *sits on a chair beside the bed, with his feet propped up on* BETA's *tricycle. The time-lapse material of the rotting prawns reduces ten days of putrefaction to sixty seconds. The light pink prawns darken, the antennae droop, the legs crumble, the carapaces blacken, a grey mould lines the segmented bodies.*

ALBA: Good Lord, Oswald, what's this?

OSWALD: Prawns on their way back.

ALBA: Way back?

OSWALD: To where they came from. Ooze, slime, murk.
(*Unknown to* ALBA, BETA, OSWALD *and* OLIVER, *and dimly seen in the semi-darkness since* OSWALD *has drawn the curtains,* VAN MEEGEREN *and his assistant* CATARINA BOLNES *are standing in the doorway, watching what is going on.* BOLNES *is wearing her ubiquitous red hat. On the screen a prawn suddenly disappears from the dish – it's the one that was taken out by* PIPE *and* VAN HOYTEN *to force down* PLATE's *throat.* ALBA *and* BETA *and* OLIVER *laugh, as do* VAN MEEGEREN *and* BOLNES *in the doorway.* OSWALD *and* ALBA *both turn to look towards the doorway to see* VAN MEEGEREN *and* BOLNES *walk out.*)

ALBA: One's still alive.

OSWALD: Someone's been tampering with my experiment.

OLIVER: Perhaps they were hungry.

OSWALD: (*Indicating the departing figures in the doorway*) Who's he?

ALBA: He's the surgeon at the hospital who removed my leg. He wants to be a painter – a Dutch painter – in fact, the Dutch painter Vermeer no less.

OSWALD: (*Disparagingly*) Vermeer only painted twenty-six paintings – and three of those are dubious.

ALBA: That's enough.

OLIVER: Obviously not – because Van Meegeren tried to paint more.

ALBA: That's his name.

OSWALD: Whose name?

ALBA: The surgeon's.

OLIVER: Pardon?

45

ALBA: Van Meegeren. He's the nephew of the faker who painted fake Vermeers.

(ALBA's *daughter,* BETA, *leaves the bed and pushing* OLIVER's *feet off the tricycle, sits on it.*)

BETA: (*To* OLIVER) Push me.

(OLIVER *gets up and pushes* BETA *down the ward.*)

OSWALD: What's his speciality?

(*The film has finished rewinding and* OSWALD *turns the projector off.*)

ALBA: Vermeer women. Van Meegeren says I look like 'The Lady Standing at the Virginal'. I suspect it's because you never see her legs – she's not standing really – she's strapped and stitched to her music stool. Van Meegeren has a great reputation for stitching.

OSWALD: Stitching?

ALBA: Yes. Suturing – sewing up wounds – operations. He's made a beautiful job on me. Look. (*She lifts up the sheet for him to see.*)

OSWALD: No. I can't. (*He turns away.*)

ALBA: (*Surprised*) Why not?

OSWALD: Because ... (*He turns back and looks hesitantly under the sheet. It's obvious he sees more than her amputated leg.*)

ALBA: You see what I mean?

OSWALD: I've seen more than that.

ALBA: Oh that. Well, that's pretty redundant now, isn't it – I mean except to pee through.

34. IN THE CORRIDOR OUTSIDE THE WARD

OLIVER *pushing* BETA *on her red tricycle passes a small service room where* VAN MEEGEREN *and* CATARINA BOLNES *are talking urgently.*

VAN MEEGEREN: I want you to make sure those two brothers don't get too close to Alba Bewick.

BOLNES: (*Angrily*) How do I do that?

VAN MEEGEREN: (*Airily*) Distract them – as you only know how.

(*Unseen by either of them,* BETA, *on her tricycle, backs into*

sight – OLIVER *is not with her – and sits and watches* VAN
MEEGEREN *and* BOLNES *with curiosity.*)
BOLNES: What's in it for me?
VAN MEEGEREN: (*Slyly*) My patient's – our patient's well-being
. . . and a continuing place in my operating theatre (*He
kisses her and fondles her breast.*) . . . and in my bed.
(*He puts his hand up her leg, lifting her skirt sufficiently for*
BETA *to see that* BOLNES *is wearing black and white striped
underwear.* BOLNES *slaps* VAN MEEGEREN's *hand down.*
BETA *stares at* VAN MEEGEREN *and* BOLNES *who stare
back.*)

35. IN THE HOSPITAL WARD
ALBA *sitting up in bed watches* OLIVER *walk down the ward
towards her.*
OLIVER: I've just thought . . . at the crash, which way was the
wind blowing? Was it coming off the buildings on the south
side or . . .
ALBA: (*Interrupting*) Oliver, for God's sake, enough – you've got
to stop – what difference does it make? You exhaust me
with your obsessions – both of you.
OLIVER: You are our only witness.
ALBA: (*With some anger*) What sort of witness was I? In searing
pain, a face full of feathers and egg yolk . . . my leg
smashed to pulp, bleeding . . . and you ask me which way
the wind was blowing.
OLIVER: I'm sorry.
ALBA: Where's Beta?
OLIVER: She's with Oswald. (*He looks crestfallen.*)
ALBA: Look, it was an accident. Five thousand accidents
happen every day – bizarre, tragic, farcical . . . they're Acts
of God fit only to amaze the survivors and irritate the
Insurance Company . . .
OLIVER: This one is different for God's sake.
ALBA: Is it?
OLIVER: . . . the wives of two zoologists die in a car driven by a

47

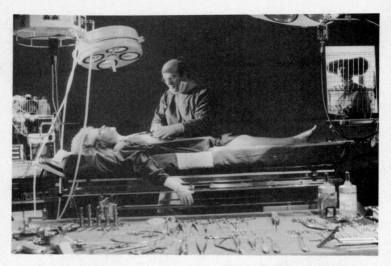

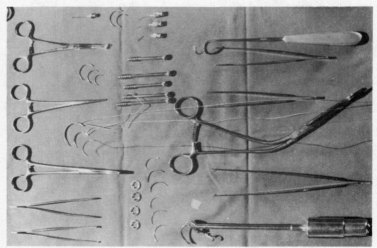

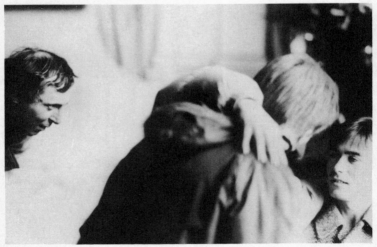

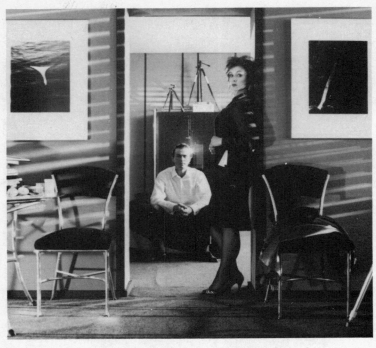

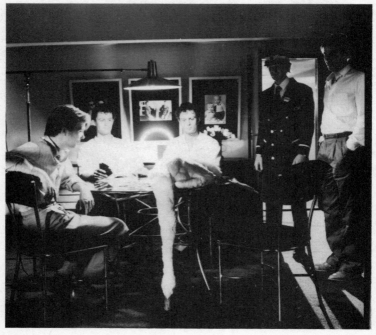

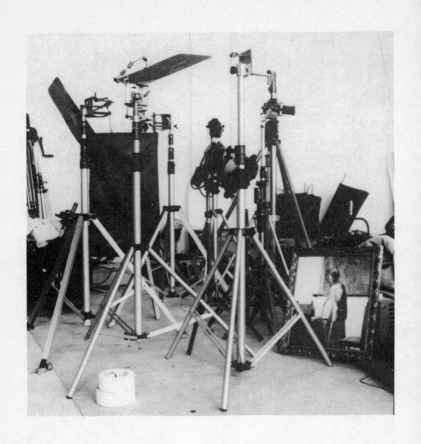

woman called Bewick who is attacked by a swan on Swan's Way?

ALBA: You are already beginning to build yourself a case for the supernatural – another set of details from the same crash could produce something completely different.
(OLIVER *lays his head on the bed.* ALBA *strokes his hair.*)
... and ... and what about me? Don't I deserve some consideration? With a daughter who can't sit still and why should she? Take her out for me will you? Van Meegeren's going to fit me with an artificial leg tomorrow. Kiss me. I haven't been kissed since your wife kissed me a month ago – kiss me on the cheek – here (*She indicates*) where she did.
(OLIVER *kisses her where requested.* ALBA *and* OLIVER *embrace. He kisses her on the mouth and she pulls his hand under the sheet.*)

36. IN THE ZOO CAFÉ
In the zoo café/restaurant with a view of some animal cages.
OLIVER *and* OSWALD *and* BETA *are seated at a café table.*
OLIVER: ... and the ostrich eats anything at all.
OSWALD: ... and buries its head in the sand when it's frightened.
OLIVER: ... and the elephant lives to be a hundred.
OSWALD: ... and never forgets a face.
(*Behind the trio at the table,* CATARINA BOLNES *sits watching them.*)
OLIVER: So you see that between us, we know everything.
BETA: You don't know everything.
OSWALD: Between us we do.
BETA: All right then. (*Looking round and seeing* CATARINA BOLNES.) You see that woman over there. What colour knickers is she wearing?
OLIVER: (*Looking around*) Well ... red ones ... to match her hat.
BETA: No she isn't.
OSWALD: (*Smiling*) How do you know?
BETA: (*Adamantly*) I know.
OSWALD: (*Smiling*) Well, Oliver, you could go and ask and find out.

BETA: Go on – ask her.

(OLIVER *resolutely goes over to ask*.)

OLIVER: Madam, excuse me. I'm sorry to bother you. I think we might just have met before. May I trouble you – in the interests of that child's education (*Pointing to* BETA) – can I ask you a few questions?

BOLNES: Like?

OLIVER: (*Now joined by* BETA *who stands close beside him*) Like – are these ostrich feathers? (*He points to her hat*.)

BOLNES: Who are you exactly? Do I know you?

OLIVER: I'm an animal behaviourist, madam.

BOLNES: Then your question doesn't sound very well informed. What animals are you a behaviourist of?

OLIVER: All animals. Madam, can I ask you a personal question?

(BETA *kicks* OLIVER *on the shin*.)

OLIVER: Madam – what colour are your knickers?

BOLNES: (*Unperturbed*) Black and white striped.

OLIVER: (*Slightly surprised at her coolness*) Thank you.

BOLNES: It's a pleasure. (*Smiling sarcastically*.)

(OLIVER *and* BETA *return to their table*.)

OLIVER: You see – black and white stripes.

BETA: You didn't know. I knew all the time.

OSWALD: You did?

BETA: Yes. I saw them yesterday.

OLIVER: Why make me go through all that?

(BOLNES *comes over to their table*.)

BOLNES: Excuse me. Just in case you don't believe me, I can show you.

OLIVER: No thank you, we believe you.

BOLNES: I insist.

OSWALD: (*Rattled and uneasy*) It's really all right thank you.

BOLNES: If you are zoologists as you claim and you pride yourselves on your powers of observation, you must continue the experiment. If you don't look at the evidence, you're cheating the child. Come with me, or I swear I'll kick this table over. (*A table nearby is loaded with glasses and china for laying the tables*.)

66

OLIVER: (*Irritated and calling her bluff*) Go on then.
(BOLNES *kicks the table over. The glass and china smash everywhere.*)
OSWALD: God!
BOLNES: Now, I'll knock this one over if you don't come with me at once.
OLIVER: Where to?
BOLNES: Just follow me.
(*Leaving* OSWALD *to deal with an irate café manager and the curious diners,* OLIVER *goes off with* BOLNES. *They enter a woman's toilet,* OLIVER *hesitating, then forcing himself to follow.* BOLNES *enters a cubicle and* OLIVER *hesitates outside.*)
BOLNES: All right, you smart zoologist. Now see for yourself.
(OLIVER *hesitates.*)
BOLNES: Go on.
(OLIVER *lifts her skirt to reveal that she has nothing on at all. He lets her skirt drop and she delivers him a smashing blow to the face.* OLIVER *staggers.*)
BOLNES: That'll cost you thirty pounds ... and another thing, Van Meegeren and I feel it is best for Alba Bewick's health if you and your precious brother stop seeing her ... before it is too late ...
OLIVER: Too late?
BOLNES: If you both feel so lonely you can't help yourselves, come and see me. (*Disdainfully*) Together if you must, and I don't tell dirty stories ...

37. VAN MEEGEREN'S SURGERY

VAN MEEGEREN'S *surgery at the hospital. There are reproductions of Vermeer paintings around the walls. The whole room looks like an empty set for a Vermeer painting – globes, maps, leather chairs.*
ALBA, BOLNES *and* VAN MEEGEREN *are in the room.* ALBA *lies on a white-sheeted bed –* VAN MEEGEREN *is attaching an artificial leg to her.*
ALBA: Don't press too hard. My back aches.
VAN MEEGEREN: Where does it ache?
ALBA: Across the hips and along the spine.

VAN MEEGEREN: Don't worry – it's a natural reaction. Let's have you in a sitting position.
(*He helps her too solicitously, touching her unnecessarily.* ALBA *is aware of it, but says nothing.*)

ALBA: Tell me, what happened to my leg?

VAN MEEGEREN: What do you mean?

ALBA: Where is it now? Have you sold it?

VAN MEEGEREN: It was incinerated.

ALBA: Where?

VAN MEEGEREN: Don't concern yourself with it.

ALBA: Where?

VAN MEEGEREN: In the hospital incinerator.

ALBA: What is your connection with the zoo?

VAN MEEGEREN: I am a veterinary consultant. Why do you ask?

ALBA: Do you perform amputations on animals?

VAN MEEGEREN: If they are necessary.

ALBA: Do you fit animals with artificial limbs?

VAN MEEGEREN: Where are these questions leading, Alba?

ALBA: Is animal surgery so different from human surgery?

VAN MEEGEREN: Dear me, as many questions as breaths. There are many similarities. Come and swing round to face me.
(ALBA *attempts to swing round.* VAN MEEGEREN *puts his hand on her thigh close to her hip ostensibly to help her.* ALBA, *as discreetly as possible, takes his hand off.*
VAN MEEGEREN *calls* BOLNES *over to him. She comes with a tape-measure. Together* VAN MEEGEREN *and* BOLNES *begin to measure* ALBA.)

ALBA: What's this for?

VAN MEEGEREN: May we? It's for a surprise.

ALBA: What sort of a surprise?

VAN MEEGEREN: Don't be alarmed. I'm sure you'll like it, and what sort of surprise will it be if we tell you?

ALBA: You take too many liberties.

VAN MEEGEREN: I do? They are all in your interest.

38. THE FISHTANKS
In a darkened room of the zoo aquarium, an adjunct of the zoo

laboratory, PIPE, OLIVER, OSWALD, *and* BETA *are standing around a large aquarium in which are swimming a large shoal of fish.*

BETA: Do you have lots of black and white fish?

PIPE: Yes.

BETA: Zebra fish?

PIPE: We also have parrot fish, elephant fish, rat fish . . . and tiger sharks.

OLIVER: You see? Fish anticipated everything that was to come. I don't know why evolution bothered to go on. Why go further?

OSWALD: There are no swan fish. (*Said with finality.*)

PIPE: (*Putting a large hand on the back of* BETA's *bare leg*) Can I interest you in an angel fish?

BETA: Is that a real fish?

OLIVER: Yes.

BETA: Can it fly?

OLIVER: If it could it still couldn't escape. It's a caged fish.

BETA: Can it swim away?

OLIVER: Where could it swim to?

BETA: (*Boldly*) The Sargasso Sea. That's where all fish go.

OLIVER: Is it?

BETA: Yes . . . that's where my mother's leg has gone.

PIPE: How's that?

BETA: It was taken there by a shark.

OSWALD: . . . called Van Meegeren perhaps?

PIPE: Who's he?

OLIVER: Just a Keeper of Legs.

PIPE: (*To* BETA) Would you like an angel fish? I'm afraid it'll cost your Uncle Oliver five pounds (*He smiles at* OLIVER.) . . . But I'm sure he won't mind.

(*The camera slowly begins to reveal a second aquarium – with angel fish in it – but they are dead. A time-lapse camera is photographing their decay. The fish are putrefying and the flesh of some of the fish has been peeled away by small crustaceans. The aquarium of dead fish is illuminated every eight seconds by a bright white light.*)

39. HOSPITAL WARD

At night, when most of the ward lights are out, OSWALD *sneaks into the hospital ward with a small black-and-white TV monitor and a video-tape deck.*

ALBA: Oswald! What are you doing here so late?

(ALBA *is pleased to see him. He sets the TV up on the trolley at the end of the bed.*)

OSWALD: Reptiles.

(OSWALD *rummages under the bed for a power socket. He turns the TV on to the 'Life on Earth' film of reptiles. Lizards fill the screen.*)

ALBA: Isn't it a bit late to be watching reptiles?

OSWALD: Four hundred million years too late.

(OSWALD *climbs on the bed beside* ALBA *and they watch for several moments.*)

ALBA: What's all this watching in aid of?

OSWALD: I'm trying to work it out.

ALBA: What out?

OSWALD: Why we've come all this way – slowly and painfully – inch by inch – fraction by fraction – second by second – so that my wife should die by a swan.

ALBA: A very personal view of evolution.

OSWALD: What have a swan and my wife in common?

ALBA: Me.

OSWALD: (*Surprised*) You?

ALBA: (*Counting on her fingers*) . . . and my car, my amputated leg . . . my lost child . . .

OSWALD: (*Much too busy with his own thoughts to worry about her pain*) Reptiles didn't die out. They grew feathers and became birds.

ALBA: So our swan was a flying lizard? Did Jupiter know that when he raped Leda?

OSWALD: He didn't rape her – she was willing.

ALBA: For God's sake Oswald – are you implying I was?

OSWALD: (*Lost by her reasoning*) What do you mean?

ALBA: You've been trying to tell me – you and Oliver – that I was responsible for your wife's death.

OSWALD: No, we haven't.

70

ALBA: Then things have suddenly changed. (OSWALD *looks crestfallen. He changes the subject by picking up the photographs of the lush landscapes from the bedside table.*)

ALBA: (*Pause*) . . . where is Oliver?

OSWALD: He's working . . . He keeps stealing snails . . . and letting butterflies free.

ALBA: (*Indicating photograph in* OSWALD'*s hand*) He ought to go there. It's full of snails and butterflies . . . (*She takes the photo from him.*) It's called L'Escargot on account of the snails – I loathed them – if you left a bicycle by the back door while you went indoors to use the toilet – when you came out – the saddle was covered in snails – licking up your sweat. I haven't been there for fifteen years . . . I'd quite like to die there. (*Brightly.*) You must go there for me. You might find my Felipe Arc-en-Ciel. (OSWALD *laughs.*) Don't laugh, I'm serious. The key is in my bag. (OSWALD *picks up* ALBA'*s handbag. He opens it to find it full of keys.*) Good Lord, Alba – which one?

ALBA: I don't know, I've forgotten. You'd better try them all. Start with this one. (*She picks one out at random.* OSWALD *laughs.*) It looks right.

OSWALD: Why on earth do you keep all these?

ALBA: I've always had them. You must never throw a key away – did you know that? Kiss me. (*He does. She pulls him towards her.*)

OSWALD: Your leg?

ALBA: (*Laughing*) What leg? . . . Don't be so sensitive. You'll be surprised what a novelty it is. (*He looks vaguely puzzled.*) . . . Come on. I want more than a kiss . . . You might like it – your brother did. (OSWALD *looks at her in surprise for a moment, then acquiesces.*

The TV screen at the bottom of the bed continues to play images of crocodiles.)

40. REPTILE HOUSE AT THE ZOO
Matching the last image. A crocodile on a sack at the zoo struggles. A wider shot reveals VAN HOYTEN *and* JOSHUA PLATE *standing*

over the crocodile. PLATE *is attaching two electrodes to the crocodile's flesh, electrocuting it.* VAN HOYTEN *watches. The crocodile convulses and dies.*

PLATE: What's the charge?

VAN HOYTEN: The charge? The charge is thirty pounds.

41. ZEBRA ENCLOSURE

At the zebra enclosure in the middle of the afternoon. The letters OO from the entrance gate letters ZOO dominate the frame. MILO *and the crippled stranger* FELIPE ARC-EN-CIEL *are watching a zebra.*

ARC-EN-CIEL: Do you think the zebra was a mistake?

MILO: (*Adamantly*) Never.

ARC-EN-CIEL: Do you think that black and white stripes are useful?

MILO: I'm sure they are. (*Smiling.*)

ARC-EN-CIEL: Since the zebra is such a beautiful animal, you'd have thought perhaps that man would have invented a fanciful hybrid, wouldn't you? You know, like a centaur, a black and white centaur perhaps – half woman, half zebra? . . . with striped breasts, ever-ready haunches and a white tail . . . and black hair?

MILO: They'd only put it in a zoo.

ARC-EN-CIEL: Next to the unicorn.

MILO: And the mermaid.

ARC-EN-CIEL: Animals are always kept for profit.

MILO: Maybe that's what they are for.

ARC-EN-CIEL: . . . and there are many ways of making a profit. (*Said with a smile.*) . . . If I had the money to own a zoo, I'd stock it with mythological animals.

MILO: And where would you find them?

ARC-EN-CIEL: I'd ask you to help me.

MILO: (*Laughing*) I'm very expensive.

42. VAN MEEGEREN'S SURGERY

Slowly zoom out from the zebra stripes of a slashed costume that VAN MEEGEREN *is wearing, that is copied from the 'Allegory of*

Painting' by Vermeer, to reveal a total image copied from the same
painting where CATARINA BOLNES *is posed naked, with her red*
hat on and holding a book and a trumpet. VAN MEEGEREN *is*
photographing her. He takes flash-light pictures reminiscent of
OSWALD DEUCE'S *time-lapse flash camera when he films decaying*
animals.

VAN MEEGEREN: Well, you don't seem to have protected Alba
from the attentions of the mooning Deuces.

BOLNES: I cannot patrol the ward like a sentry.

VAN MEEGEREN: You could surely offer more attractive
alternatives than a woman with one leg? ... (*Pause.*)
Would they be interested in a woman with no legs at all?

BOLNES: (*Throwing down the book and the trumpet*) Since you
obviously have more interest in her than you do in me, you
ought to be able to answer that question yourself.

43. CROCODILE HOUSE AT THE ZOO
OLIVER, OSWALD, BETA *with* ALBA *in a bright chromium-plated*
wheelchair, are grouped around the crocodile enclosure looking at the
crocodiles who move slowly in turgid water. A water-feed splashes
regularly into the gloomy water. Somewhere in the background an
attendant is washing out an enclosure. The sounds of a hose running
and of the man whistling echo in the semi-dark space – semi-dark
because it's raining heavily outside – the rain running down the
slanted window glass. The interior is slightly spooky. OLIVER *and*
OSWALD, *developing their rapport with one another in public, make*
affectionate play of ALBA's *condition.* OLIVER *directs* BETA's
attention to the crocodiles.

OLIVER: Now Captain Hook had only one leg.

BETA: (*Sharply contradicting him*) It was his arm.

OLIVER: ... and Long John Silver?

ALBA: They were both fictional – so they don't count.

OSWALD: ... and Victor Hugo's father?

ALBA: He *wrote* fiction, so *he* doesn't count.

OSWALD: It was a cork leg.

ALBA: Really? (*With sarcasm*) I wonder if he had as much
trouble as I'm having in getting it fitted. Next time you two
must come with me.

OLIVER: Why?

ALBA: To protect me from unnecessary attentions.

OSWALD: You're imagining it.

OLIVER: (*To* BETA) Pinocchio's legs were wooden, and Toulouse Lautrec ...

ALBA: (*Interrupting*) He had legs – they were just a little short.

OSWALD: Now *his* father kept horses.

OLIVER: So ... Marie Antoinette's father kept pigs, and look what happened to her.

OSWALD: Marie Antoinette's father didn't keep pigs.

OLIVER: Well, somebody's father did.

ALBA: You two are improving, aren't you? Who'd have thought you knew one another? (*Said with a bantering smile at their talking double-act.*)

(BETA *pushes her mother off in the wheelchair, leaving the two brothers standing by the crocodile enclosure. They both look hard at one another. There is a pause and they look at the crocodiles.*)

OSWALD: Well? Shall we jump in now or later?

OLIVER: They don't look very hungry.

OSWALD: What would we taste like?

OLIVER: Crocodiles have no taste-buds. Besides, grief doesn't flavour anything – it's just sour.

(*The brothers stare into the crocodile enclosure.* PLATE *comes up discreetly behind them. He is dripping wet in a soaked raincoat. His clothes make a puddle on the floor.*)

PLATE: Excuse me.

(*The brothers turn round.*)

(*Speaking to* OSWALD) Can I have a word with you?

OSWALD: Go ahead.

PLATE: (*With an insinuating grin*) Would you not prefer to speak to me alone?

OSWALD: No.

PLATE: Dear me. Grief can be a great healer. (*Mainly to Oswald.*) I understand you may be looking for dead animals?

OSWALD: I may be.

PLATE: What exactly are you looking for?

OSWALD: A reptile.

PLATE: Wouldn't something much larger do?

OSWALD: Not yet.

PLATE: Would a crocodile do?

OSWALD: It might, but I'm unlikely to find one.

PLATE: How much would you pay?

OSWALD: Pay? I haven't thought.

PLATE: I understand, with the insurance money, that you are
  not badly off?

OLIVER: That's none of your business.

PLATE: (*Brusquely*) Forty pounds?

OSWALD: That seems a lot.

PLATE: Thirty-five pounds? (*He pulls the crocodile corpse from
  under his dripping raincoat.*)

OLIVER: Where did you get that?

PLATE: In a zoo community of seven thousand animals there are
  deaths every day. Crocodiles are not immortal.
  (OSWALD *takes out his wallet and counts out the money.
  Handing it over, he takes the crocodile and tries to hide it under
  his coat. It is too big.* OLIVER *takes off his jacket, sniffs the
  corpse and the two of them wrap it up.*)

PLATE: (*Smiling*) If you should get more ambitious, I would be
  pleased to help. On an exclusive basis of course.
  (PLATE *leaves.*)

OSWALD: Everybody in this zoo has something to sell. Why are
  we always the buyers?

44. VAN MEEGEREN'S SURGERY
ALBA, OLIVER, OSWALD, VAN MEEGEREN, BOLNES *and* MILO
are in the 'Vermeer' decorated room we have seen before. ALBA *is
being fitted with her artificial leg.* MILO *and* BOLNES *are further
back in the room.*

VAN MEEGEREN: (*To* ALBA) Now try walking to the armchair.

ALBA: You must hold me.

VAN MEEGEREN: Oswald, Oliver – make yourselves useful,
  now you're here. Come and steer Alba to the chair. Follow
  the line on the carpet.
  (*The brothers gingerly guide* ALBA *across the floor – her long*

white dress is open down the front, exposing her white silk underwear. The brothers are timorous and excited by turns by the proximity of ALBA – *her flesh and her elegant metal leg.)*

ALBA: (*In a low voice*) I'm not sure, Oliver, if you're helping or hindering.

OLIVER: I'm not really sure why I'm here at all.

ALBA: You're both here to look after me.

(VAN MEEGEREN *comes closer.*)

If you took larger steps, Oswald, I needn't lean so far to the right.

VAN MEEGEREN: Don't be so dependent on him then. Take larger steps yourself.

ALBA: A mechanical leg is a fake.

VAN MEEGEREN: So? What isn't a fake? Try lifting the leg higher. Fake or not it could get you to Amsterdam to see a real Vermeer.

(ALBA *reaches the sofa where she half falls, half sits, ineptly aided by the Deuce brothers.*)

VAN MEEGEREN: Now, in honour of your entourage (*Heavily sarcastic*) – since we must make their presence enjoyable, else why are they here? – the surprise. De Milo, *my* seamstress, (*The Deuce brothers raise their eyebrows at one another*) on my instructions, has made you a dress. (*He clicks his fingers.* MILO *and* BOLNES *bring over a long, wide-skirted dress in yellow, white and black.*) It is a copy in every detail of the one worn by Madame Van Ees in both 'The Concert' and 'The Music-lesson'. (*He gestures to the wall where details of the dress in reproduction are hung.*) We now nearly have the entire wardrobe seen in Vermeer's paintings.

MILO: (*With a smile*) Including the fakes.

VAN MEEGEREN: (*To* ALBA) Try it on.

ALBA: I came for an artificial leg, not an artificial dress.

VAN MEEGEREN: Just to please me. Milo, help Alba with her dress. Have you two met?

ALBA: (*Smiling generously*) I know enough, Milo, to know that you favour black and plan to earn your living writing. I know a publisher. You must come and tell me some dirty stories. (*Laughing.*)

MILO: (*Laughing*) Well, what would you like? I can tell you about what Venus did to the unicorn in Beardsley's 'Under the Hill'. He got paid sixty guineas. What was sixty guineas worth do you think?

VAN MEEGEREN: (*Said with some admonishment*) Milo, can you help Alba.

MILO: In this room, as you can see, I am only useful holding pins.

VAN MEEGEREN: Alba, try the dress on.

ALBA: Do I really have to?

BOLNES: (*Under her breath and with some vehemence to* VAN MEEGEREN) That dress was for me.

VAN MEEGEREN: Rubbish, my dear. Go and amuse those two simpletons. I'll see to Alba.

(BOLNES *gives* VAN MEEGEREN *a withering look and sits herself on the sofa.*)

VAN MEEGEREN: Come and sit here at the piano. Can you play?

ALBA: Nothing very complicated.

(VAN MEEGEREN *and* MILO *assist* ALBA *to the piano-stool where they drape and swathe her dress.* ALBA *plays the 'Teddy-Bear's Picnic'.* MILO *busies herself with pins in her mouth.* VAN MEEGEREN *brings books from the shelves and he and* MILO *compare details from the Vermeer painting.*)

VAN MEEGEREN: It needs a tuck here . . . there's not enough spread. What a pity about the hair.

(VAN MEEGEREN *and* MILO *go to consult further books in the corner of the room. The Deuce brothers approach* ALBA, *who looks miserable. Tears start to well up in her eyes.*)

ALBA: (*Whispering*) Get me out of here. It's terrible.

OSWALD: What's so terrible?

ALBA: I'm an excuse for medical experiments and art theory. You must get me out of here and out of the hospital.

OLIVER: They're trying to help you.

ALBA: Help me, for God's sake. What are you thinking? I'm stitched and sewn to the music-stool. Look. I'm imprisoned.

(ALBA *is indeed pinned and tacked into a rigid position.*)

45. BIRDS FILM

To contrast ALBA's *imprisonment and last line, the screen is filled with a mass of screeching, flying birds in Part Six of the 'Life on Earth' film series.* MILO *and* JOSHUA PLATE *are sitting in the zoo viewing theatre watching the film, though* PLATE *is more interested in* MILO. *In bemused frustration at* MILO's *refusal to extend her services in his direction, he says:*

PLATE: Why not? (MILO *merely smiles.*)

46. L'ESCARGOT

On exactly the same image of L'Escargot that is depicted on the photographs beside ALBA's *bed – only greener now and moving with windblown vegetation –* OLIVER *and* OSWALD DEUCE *walk slowly into the frame. They swat at insects, chew grass, pick at seed heads. They are naked to the waist and wear opaque black sunglasses.*

OLIVER: It's beautiful.

OSWALD: Does Alba really know what she's got here?

OLIVER: I'm sure of it.

OSWALD: Does she really know what she's doing?

OLIVER: She's trying to start all over again.

OSWALD: By sleeping with two brothers who can't tell the difference between pleasure and grief and take advantage of her loneliness?

OLIVER: My impression was she was taking advantage of *our* loneliness.

OSWALD: So who's benefitting most out of this mutual exploitation?

OLIVER: For the moment I am.

OSWALD: Why you?

OLIVER: Because I'm enjoying this. (*Waving his arm over the garden.*) You're here, but worried about exploitation, and Alba's not here but in bed without a leg.

(OLIVER *stoops and lifts a broken branch. Underneath are a mass of snails.*)

ALBA *is triumphantly wheeled in her wheelchair – with her eyes bandaged – through the doors of a suite in a smart hotel. Sunlight fills the room. There are cut flowers and champagne laid out on a trolley.* OLIVER *pushes the wheelchair;* OSWALD *carries the suitcases;* BETA *carries her angel fish in a glass bowl. They stop in the centre of the sitting-room.*

OSWALD: There. We have not found you a Felipe Arc-en-Ciel, but we have found you an apartment. Take off your blindfold. (*She does so.*) Now you'll be safe from Art and Medicine.

(BETA *runs from room to room and then runs into the bathroom. She turns on the hot tap.* BETA *runs the bath, testing the hot water carefully. She empties her fish into the bath.* BETA *drags* OSWALD *into the bathroom.*)

BETA: Quick, she's got to be kept warm. If angels get cold, they die.

OSWALD: What makes you think it's a she?

BETA: Because she's going to have babies.

OSWALD: Oh!

(*He goes back into the sitting-room*).

OLIVER: Let's celebrate. (*He pours champagne.*)

ALBA: And you'd better fill the glasses up.

OSWALD: What do you mean? Do you like the view?

ALBA: (*Laughing*) It's certainly convenient for the zoo. It looks very expensive and a little vulgar. So who's going to pay for all this?

OSWALD: We are.

(OLIVER *puts a record on the record-player. It's a version of the 'Teddy Bear's Picnic' – the classic one.*)

OLIVER: And here's a reminder of how it really goes . . .

ALBA: I see – exchanging one prison for another – but the music is still the same. So I'm to be a kept woman?

OLIVER: (*Laughing*) Not so you'd notice.

ALBA: Will I be able to escape if I want to?

OLIVER: Of course. You know I don't believe in cages.

ALBA: (*Smiling*) Suppose I don't want to escape?

OSWALD: Good grief, Alba, you're free to come and go as you please.

ALBA: Good. I just want to get that straight. They clip the wings of birds in the zoo . . .

OLIVER: But they always grow again.

ALBA: Now that wasn't such a bright thing to say in the circumstances, was it? (*Looking at her leglessness.*)

OLIVER: (*Contritely*) I'm sorry.

ALBA: Who has the keys?

OSWALD: You can have the keys.

OLIVER: Keys aren't in it. Look, you're as free as a bird.

ALBA: (*Laughing*) Just like Leda. Prove I'm as free as a bird.

OLIVER: Prove it? All right, all right. (*He thinks rapidly.*) You just sit on your balcony at nine o'clock tomorrow morning and I'll show you how easy it is to free birds.
(BETA, *in enthusiastic delight at her fish, gets into the bath with it; fully dressed.*)

ALBA: That sounds interesting. (*Laughing.*) Now let's see how all that changes in the face of new evidence. Have another drink.

OLIVER: Thank you.

ALBA: You may need it.

OSWALD: I may?

ALBA: You may. (*She clears her throat.*) *I* am about to become a mother and *you* are about to become a father . . . or fathers. (*The gramophone record stops.*)

OSWALD: You what?

OLIVER: You are?

ALBA: I am.

OSWALD: Good Lord.

ALBA: Why not?

OLIVER: You can?

ALBA: Of course. (*Indignantly.*) Is leglessness a form of contraception?

OSWALD: (*Dazed*) I'm not sure.

ALBA: (*Taken aback by his ingenuousness*) You're not sure?

OSWALD: (*Not convincingly*) I'm delighted.

ALBA: You're delighted? A pregnant cripple and you're
     delighted? Think of what it will do to my sense of balance.
OSWALD: It might help; give you more stability.
ALBA: Then you recommend it? Recommendation's one thing, a
     womb on crutches is another.
OSWALD: So who's the father? (*Said with hesitation.*)
ALBA: Well, well, well. Why don't you discuss it between
     yourselves?
OLIVER: Don't you know?
ALBA: Good Lord. An animal behaviourist needs to ask such
     questions? As far as I'm concerned you both are.
OSWALD: But . . .
ALBA: No buts . . . you're brothers, aren't you? What's a few
     spermatozoa among brothers.

48. THE DECAY OF THE ANGEL FISH
OSWALD DEUCE's *decay experiment with the angel fish . . . ten or
so days of rotting condensed into twenty seconds. Two angel fish
corpses floating in a brightly lit aquarium grow white, are attacked
by crustaceans, putrefy and the bones are picked clean.*

49. RELEASE OF THE FLAMINGOES
At night. MILO *and* OLIVER *are among the bird cages and
enclosures. They stand up against a tall wire-netting gate, struggling
to pick the padlock on the flamingo enclosure.*
MILO: . . . Do you have a flat piece of plastic?
OLIVER: No.
MILO: Have you got a sharpened pencil?
OLIVER: No.
MILO: (*Sarcastically*) You *are* well equipped. (*She stoops to take
     off her shoes.*) Here hold these.
     (MILO *returns to pick the lock industriously,* OLIVER *stands
     and holds her shoes.*)
OLIVER: Why are you doing this for me?
MILO: Because you're going to pay me generously; and I like
     the gesture . . . and you still might find me a publisher.

OLIVER: One wants a publisher and the other wants a rainbow.
MILO: A rainbow?
OLIVER: A French rainbow – a Mr Felipe Arc-en-Ciel.
MILO: (*Laughing*) We must give my fictitious publisher a name.
How about . . . (*She thinks.*) . . . Mr Ted Chimera?
(*The gate swings open with a clang.*)

50. FLAMINGOES IN THE STREET
A street full of flamingoes in the early morning sun. In the balcony-room of ALBA'*s Zoo Hotel apartment, the interior is shadowy.*
OSWALD *and* BETA *are sitting at a table cutting and glueing coloured photographs of animals.* OSWALD *is glueing and matching together pairs of the same animal – two snakes, two birds, two fish – twinning them to make a logical two-animal creature. On the table is a black-and-white TV set. The TV plays Part Seven from the 'Life on Earth' series – showing zebras.* ALBA *and* OLIVER *are sitting on a chaise-longue in the sun on the balcony.* JEROME FALLAST *stands behind them.*
FALLAST: (*Smiling*) Oliver – invigorating as the sight may be to
you – (*looking at the flamingoes in the street*) perhaps you can
tell me if you know anything about their escape?
OLIVER: (*Smiling back*) Do you think I should know?
FALLAST: I understand that you are critical about my custody of
birds?
(*Inside the room,* BETA *is watching* OSWALD *cut and glue two
birds together.*)
BETA: My fish is lonely.
OSWALD: Well, I'll show you what to do. Come with me.
(*They troop out to the bathroom,* OSWALD *picking up a hand
mirror from the table as he leaves.* OSWALD *puts the mirror in
the bath water, moving around the fish until he has managed to
catch its reflection successfully.*)
OSWALD: There you are, a mirror image. It's not that
impossible to find.
(*Back on the balcony.*)
OLIVER: The flamingo, Jerome, lives on crustaceans. The
richer the diet, the pinker the feathers. Your birds are too
pale.

FALLAST: Fresh prawns are rather difficult to keep – as I'm sure you understand, Oliver.

OLIVER: The flamingo enclosure is ten feet by twelve. You have 123 birds, which gives each bird one square foot.

FALLAST: Flamingoes normally roost standing on one another's feet.

OLIVER: Flamingoes never experience a temperature lower than five degrees centigrade.

FALLAST: Nor do they respect traffic signals. Your fugitive, cold and anaemic flamingoes do not look terribly at home waiting for a taxi. (*He looks over the balcony.*)

OLIVER: You've got it wrong. They're waiting for a bus ... to Africa.

FALLAST: (*Sarcastically*) How charming.

(*With considerable aplomb, a very smartly dressed* VENUS DE MILO *walks down the street among the flamingoes. Moving to look,* ALBA *slides along the* chaise-longue, *leaving her shoes behind.* VENUS *looks up and waves.* ALBA *and* OLIVER *wave back. Four zoo-keepers are coming down the street with nets and staves and sections of wattle-fencing and they block off a section of road to trap the flamingoes.*

In the interior of the room, OSWALD *and* BETA *are pairing birds.*)

BETA: They look like twins. Could they fly like that, do you think? Joined together like that?

OSWALD: They could learn.

(*On the balcony,* FALLAST *bows and prepares to leave.*)

FALLAST: Oliver, a warning. Snails, butterflies and now birds have escaped from the zoo. I take them all to be irresponsible acts, increasing in irresponsibility. It is possible to make allowances for your behaviour.

OLIVER: You are jumping to too many conclusions, Jerome. I am employed to *watch* animals ...

FALLAST: I cannot prove that you are responsible, Oliver, but I am sure my suspicions are not too far from the truth. Be careful. (*He leaves.*)

OLIVER: Well, I did it.

ALBA: So you did. What did you do it for?

OLIVER: To please you. To please myself. To please my wife,

who hated zoos, and to show that pedant he runs a phoney zoo.

(BETA *comes out on to the balcony.*)

BETA: Can I have one?

ALBA: One what?

BETA: A flamingo.

OLIVER: Only if you can catch one.

BETA: They're prettier than swans.

51. IN THE TIME-LAPSE LABORATORY

In the time-lapse lab, OSWALD *has made some attempt to 'regularize' his decay experiments. He has set the crocodile against 'graph-boards' – blackboards ruled like graph paper – to attempt to measure the change in shape and size of the decaying crocodile. The crocodile is laid belly uppermost in some semblance (remote resonance) to a human on its back. The crocodile is decaying.*

52. AT OSWALD'S APARTMENT

In the living room, the two DEUCE BROTHERS *sit in the gloom playing a four-handed game of cards with a pair of twins.* OSWALD *gets up to answer a ring at the door. He returns with* JOSHUA PLATE *who carries a dead swan.* PLATE *throws it down on the card-table.*

53. ZOO HOTEL APARTMENT

ALBA *is lying on her bed in the sunlit room. The space where her right leg should be is very apparent, under the thin white sheet. The two brothers sit on the far side of the bed. In the foreground* BETA *sits on the floor playing with a soft toy zebra. The child has naked legs and stretches them out towards the camera.* BETA *puts the record 'An Elephant Never Forgets' on her record player.*

ALBA: I've got to go back to hospital.

OLIVER: Why?

ALBA: I'm going to lose the other one.

OSWALD: Other what?

ALBA: This one. (*She sits up and flips back the sheet to reveal her leg to the groin.* OLIVER *makes to cover the leg up.*) What's the matter with you – it looks all right, doesn't it? (*She*

84

takes OLIVER's *hand and runs it down her leg, the flesh is smooth, supple and beautiful. She guides* OLIVER's *hand up to her upper thigh.*)

OLIVER: Of course it does – what's wrong with it? (*He makes to take his hand away, a little abashed at her forthrightness.*)

ALBA: It's got to go.

OSWALD: You're joking? You can't be serious?

ALBA: (*Sarcastically*) 'You're pulling my leg'?
(*There is a long silent pause while all three contemplate the beautiful leg. The record stops playing.*)

ALBA: It's dying.

OSWALD: How can it be dying?

ALBA: It's all on its own. It's lonely. (*She weeps. There is another silent pause.*)

ALBA: (*Suddenly and brightly*) You never see a female leg in a Vermeer. Have you noticed? Do you think it's a conspiracy by Van Meegeren? It's Van Meegeren who says it's got to come off. He says it's the shock to the spine. I'm getting so that I can hardly move. Feel it. It's cold, don't you think? Could you both love this leg as much as me? It's the only leg I've got left. How much of your body can you lose and still recognize yourself? Two legs look so good together, don't you think? They complement one another – it's obvious they were made for each other.

OLIVER: (*Looking at his brother*) Like us.

OSWALD: Like your legs, Alba, we are complementary.

ALBA: Of course you are. What's the name of that piece of you at the back of the knee?

OSWALD: It hasn't got a name.

ALBA: Then I won't miss it.

OLIVER: Lots of other features haven't got common names. This (*He points*) small piece of gristle that separates the nostrils.

OSWALD: It also keeps them together.

ALBA: Why do we have to have two nostrils? Why do we have to have two of everything?

OSWALD: Symmetry is all.

OLIVER: We're twins.

85

ALBA: I know you are.
(*There is a long pause.*)
ALBA: (*Suddenly breaking the silence*) Just because you've chosen now to reveal your amazing secret doesn't mean I have to be surprised.
OLIVER: Who told you?
ALBA: No one. I guessed. Not even your wives told me.
OSWALD: They didn't know.
ALBA: They didn't know. Come on.
OSWALD: They didn't know. They knew we were brothers but they were never told that we were twins.
ALBA: Well now, *that* is a surprise ... (*She returns to her greater problem.*) ... Well – they can't torture me any more by burning straws between my toes. I can't be tickled to death on the soles of my feet. I can't be kneecapped or get housemaid's knee ...
OLIVER: ... or get athlete's foot ...
ALBA: ... or a verruca.
OSWALD: You can get verrucas on your hands.
ALBA: Say good-bye to my leg, both of you.
OLIVER: (*Against his better judgement*) Good-bye, leg.
ALBA: Go on, Oswald.
OSWALD: (*Lamely*) Good-bye, leg.
ALBA: Kiss it. It needs a send-off. Here and here. (*She points to her knee and her thigh.*) Poor leg.
(*Throwing herself violently back on the bed, she bursts into long, heart-rending, breathless sobs.* BETA, *watches, expressionless.*)

54. HOSPITAL OPERATING THEATRE
In the hospital operating theatre, surrounded by operating staff, in a set-up very similar to the scene in the Prologue, ALBA, *identified unmistakably by her red hair, lies on the operating table. At her head, partly masked by anaesthetist's equipment, is* CATARINA BOLNES. *She sits with combs and scissors and is preparing* ALBA'S *hair in the style of Madame de Guys – the sitter in many of Vermeer's paintings. For reference,* BOLNES *has, in front of her, copies – large and small – of Vermeer paintings. With great interest,*

VAN MEEGEREN, *holding aloft a pair of tweezers, in the act of suturing, bends over to see what* BOLNES *is accomplishing. He indicates that she should turn the reproductions around so that he can compare the differences.*

55. ZOO LABORATORY
The decay of the lizard on time-lapse film. Four weeks of decay are condensed into twenty-five seconds.

56. IN THE HOSPITAL WARD
ALBA *discovers that her hair has been combed and teased by* BOLNES *into the image of one of Vermeer's sitters. She shouts and curses and tears the ribbons from her hair. Very weak from the operation, she falls back on the bed, weeping.*

57. ZOO HOTEL – ALBA'S APARTMENT – THE BEDROOM
Night time. Late at night. A meal has been set up on trays and trolleys: silver coffee-pots, silver tureens, fruits, wine, etc. There are trays on the bed and the floor. ALBA *and* OSWALD *have just finished eating and are awaiting the return of* OLIVER. *There is music on a gramophone. Several separate lamps create different atmospheres in different parts of the room. There is a knock on the door and the immediate entrance of* OLIVER. *He looks hot and excited.* ALBA *is noticeably pregnant.*

OLIVER: Come to the window. Turn out the light.
> (OLIVER *walks across the room to the window. He picks up a slice of cake and a cup of coffee on his way, stuffing the cake into his mouth.* OSWALD *switches out the lamp that illuminates the window area and joins his brother at the window.*)

ALBA: What are you watching?

OLIVER: It's a convalescence present – to celebrate your return to the Zoo Hotel . . . I've turned out the rhino. It followed me to the corner . . .

OSWALD: . . . and then you abandoned it?

OLIVER: It'll be all right.

OSWALD: Supposing it attacks someone?

OLIVER: It won't. It's short-sighted.

OSWALD: God . . . who's helping who?

(*With* ALBA *in the bed behind them, quietly eating grapes, the two brothers strain to look out of the window into the darkened street. Outside, the rhino, its head up, stands in the middle of the street in the moonlight. It sniffs the urban night breeze. The night is very quiet; only the muted sound of distant traffic and a far-off nocturnal train.*)

OSWALD: It's standing in its own shadow. High noon in the Kalahari scrub.

ALBA: Carry me to the window. I've never been to Africa.
(*The brothers carefully lift* ALBA *out of the bed and carry her to the window seat. The three watch out of the window. The position and the occasion suggest intimacy.* OLIVER *takes advantage of it and kisses* ALBA. *A predatory beginning.* ALBA *offers her other cheek to* OSWALD, *who, more hesitatingly than his brother, kisses her.* ALBA *puts her arms around them both.*)

ALBA: The rhino seems able to look after itself . . . take me back to bed . . . and come and join me . . .
(*The brothers carry* ALBA *back to bed, remove the plates and trays from the bed and undress,* ALBA *watching them. They undress in a shadowy part of the room and get into the bed. The three in the bed begin to make love, without competitiveness – the two brothers cosseting the legless, pregnant woman.*
Out in the street, the rhino is cautiously approached by a group of zoo keepers – eager to recapture it. ALBA, OLIVER *and* OSWALD *sit up in the large double bed. They drink champagne.*)

ALBA: Now, how about changing sides?

OSWALD: No, I'm happy on the left.

ALBA: That sounds political – at the very least prohibitive.

OSWALD: On the contrary. I know my place exactly and feel very comfortable in it. Though it's possibly only tonight for the first time that I am prepared to acknowledge it.

ALBA: Know your place?

OSWALD: Since before I was three.

ALBA: You have a long memory.

OLIVER: . . . and a few scars to prove it.

ALBA: Prove it?

OSWALD: Below the ear . . .

OLIVER: At the shoulder...

OSWALD: On the hip...

OLIVER: And along the shin.

(*The sheet is thrown back to exhibit the scars which are faint but visible.*)

ALBA: Oswald and Oliver – Siamese twins. Why haven't you acknowledged it before?

OLIVER: Maternal advice.

OSWALD: Live normally, say nothing and nobody will ever know.

ALBA: But it's something special to shout about, isn't it?

OSWALD: Was it?

OLIVER: Freaks and rarities used to be kept in circuses. Now we're all civilized, they're kept in zoos.

OSWALD: Our mother didn't like the idea of us being a rare species...

OLIVER: ... in a zoo.

(*The aftermath of the rhino's presence in the street. An overturned car. A pile of gently steaming rhino dung. The distant wail of sirens.*)

ALBA: How strange that a rhinoceros should have reunited you.

OLIVER: It's going to have to pay for it by recapture.

OSWALD: It was no rhinoceros; it was you that reunited us.

ALBA: How am I going to have to pay for it?

Running around the block – the two brothers tied together – small figures with long shadows in the early light – approach a dead dog on a zebra crossing – a Dalmatian with prominent markings – the same dog that was seen in the very first shot of the film. Sitting on the kerb are the dog's owners, a boy and a girl aged around ten.

58. ZOO LABORATORY

In the time-lapse laboratory, there are at least a dozen cameras staggered across the large spaces – alternately light and dark. Each set has different characteristics – each flickers with a regular flash – some at eight, some at ten, some at twelve seconds. Some of the lights flash synchronously with the sound of a bell or a buzzer. The camera tracks down the laboratory past OSWALD's experiments, past the decayed body of the lizard, the rotten swan, to the corpse of the

Dalmatian which OSWALD *is arranging, with the children beside him watching.* VAN HOYTEN *enters.* OSWALD *sprays the dog and switches on the camera flash.*

VAN HOYTEN: Where did you get that dog?

OSWALD: It died on a zebra crossing . . . which should make it immune from prosecution . . . and is it you that drives a black Citroen?

VAN HOYTEN: That dog should not be here. It's not a zoo animal.

OSWALD: Will you shut up, you're distressing these children. It's their dog and I'm going to immortalize it for them.

VAN HOYTEN: It's probably diseased.

OSWALD: Of course it's not diseased.

VAN HOYTEN: You've no right to use zoo equipment on any old animal you find in the street.

OSWALD: Especially not a black and white one? . . . knocked down by a malicious driver? What's special, Hoyten, about black and white animals that you have to reserve your special animosity for them?

VAN HOYTEN: (*Smiling*) Nothing.

OSWALD: What did you say?

VAN HOYTEN: (*Viciously*) Unless you pay me £200 for the use of that dog . . .

OSWALD: Hoyten – it is not yours to sell . . . and if I can prove you killed it, it's you who will be paying . . .

VAN HOYTEN: . . . I'm going to report this misuse of zoo property to Fallast.

OSWALD: You do that.

(VAN HOYTEN *leaves in a hurry.*)

BOY: This dog always refused to come into this zoo.

(OSWALD *draws up three canvas-backed chairs and motions the children to sit down. They do so. The camera light-flash lights up their faces.*)

OSWALD: I like it in here. I sit here for hours. It's like sitting amongst lighthouses, each lighthouse giving you a bearing on lost spaces of time . . . there are tens of thousands of photographs taken here, all taken very patiently, because decay can be very slow . . . (*Relapsing into absentminded*

reverie.) ... Ten months for a human body ... they say ...
(*The children sit wide-eyed watching their dog, their faces
regularly illuminated by the flashing camera.*)

59. THE ZEBRA ENCLOSURE
At noon. The letters of ZOO are shining in the sun. MILO *and*
FELIPE ARC-EN-CIEL *stand in the shadow of a heavily leafed tree
by the zebra enclosure.*
MILO: Why are zebras always given for the last letter in the
    alphabet?
ARC-EN-CIEL: Can you think of a better word?
MILO: (*Laughing*) What did they use for Z before people knew
    that zebras existed?
ARC-EN-CIEL: That was so long ago nobody needed an
    alphabet. (*Smiling.*) I think the letter Z was invented
    especially for zebras.
MILO: What is your name?
ARC-EN-CIEL: (*He smiles*) Why, Felipe Arc-en-Ciel.

60. L'ESCARGOT
The brothers take BETA *and* ALBA *to L'Escargot. They row down
the L'Escargot stream.* ALBA *is in her wheelchair in the rowing boat.*
ALBA: If you've got any control over it, I want to be buried
    here.
OLIVER: You can't.
ALBA: Why not?
OSWALD: It's not consecrated ground.
ALBA: Well, we could make it consecrated ground. I'll be
    cremated and you can scatter my ashes here.
OLIVER: Snails don't like ashes.
ALBA: Then they'll just have to put up with them. By the way,
    you still owe me a cripple.
OSWALD: Pardon?
ALBA: I said you could only come here if you found me a cripple
    to cherish ... and I expect you to find him before I deliver.
    (*Holding her stomach.*)
OLIVER: (*Laughing*) Are we likely to find him for you, if you
    intend to make him push us out?

91

ALBA: Push you out? (*Still holding her stomach.*) You're both zoologists. I want you to be there when I deliver, it might cure you of your obsession with decay. Keep looking.

61. DECAY OF THE SWAN

Time-lapse film shows OSWALD *moving towards a greater 'scientific' use of his decay time-lapse photography. He has attempted to codify putrefaction by placing the swan in a box, marked off with graduations: a three-dimensional grid marked off in centimetre squares – white lines on matt black. The swan decays, shrinks, decomposes. Four weeks of decomposition is reduced to twenty-five seconds.*

62. IN MILO'S BASEMENT APARTMENT

MILO *is sitting on her sofa. She is stitching a mannish-looking black and white suit. She is sitting in her underwear.* OSWALD *and* OLIVER *are sitting beside her drinking tea.*

MILO: I have this new story about the origin of the Sphinx ... you know, what walks on four legs in the morning, two legs at noon and three legs in the afternoon? Do you think Alba will like it? It's yours for £25.

OSWALD: We want you to make us a suit.

MILO: I know ... plenty of measuring inside leg.

OLIVER: God. You've got a one-track mind. (*The brothers sit down on either side of* MILO *on the sofa.*)

MILO: You mean you have two? One each?

OSWALD: We want you to make us a suit.

MILO: There are plenty of respectable tailors.

OLIVER: A three-piece suit.

MILO: Oh. Who's the third part for?

OSWALD: All three parts are for us, Milo, but are you capable of handling the inside arms?

(MILO *laughs and puts her arms around the two brothers, pinning their arms.*)

MILO: All right, I'll strike a bargain. Get me a story published and I'll even make the underwear that goes with the suit – and the hat. (*Laughter.*) And there is someone I've found who you must meet.

63. IN ALBA'S APARTMENT AT THE ZOO HOTEL

ALBA, *very pregnant, is reading a letter by the light of a window. The composition and feeling is similar to Vermeer's 'Woman Reading a Letter'.* VAN MEEGEREN *creeps up behind her and makes her jump. He rips the wrapping-paper off a framed reproduction of Vermeer's 'Woman Reading a Letter'.*

ALBA: Don't ever do that. A legless woman has no sense of balance.

VAN MEEGEREN: Not even a pregnant one? I've brought you a present.

ALBA: Did Vermeer ever have a life of his own? (*Exasperated.*)

VAN MEEGEREN: Did his sitters?

ALBA: I'm told his wife never sat for him.

VAN MEEGEREN: Vermeer's wife, Catarina Bolnes, gave him fourteen children.

ALBA: It strikes me that lying down for your husband is less tedious than sitting up for a friend.

VAN MEEGEREN: My Catarina Bolnes is barren.

ALBA: *Your* Catarina Bolnes?

VAN MEEGEREN: She changed her name by deedpoll because I asked her to.

ALBA: Good Lord. (*Mockingly*) What an influence you must have.

VAN MEEGEREN: (*Sharply*) I understand that you are now called Leda?

ALBA: It is an affectionate joke with no strings.

VAN MEEGEREN: I'm glad.

ALBA: You're glad?

VAN MEEGEREN: Alba, I've been very close to you . . . on the operating-table . . . with just a little encouragement from you I could be as close again. (*He gets on the bed and puts his arm around her shoulder.*)

ALBA: Take your arm off my shoulder.

VAN MEEGEREN: Come on, Alba, what excitements can a legless woman come by?

ALBA: Enough to make your attentions superfluous. Get off the bed, Meegeren, you fake, your shoes are muddy.

VAN MEEGEREN: I can always take my shoes off.

ALBA: If that was calculated to be cruel, you certainly don't
know how to make an appeal even on the poorest level.
Now leave, and take Vermeer with you. (*Indicating the
painting.*) *Your* Catarina Bolnes is waiting for you, barren
or not.
(VAN MEEGEREN'*s assistant is standing by the apartment
door.*)

64. THE ZEBRA ENCLOSURE
*A man and a zebra are standing on cobbled stones next to a zoo
building. They are partly shadowed. The zebra's tail, rump and
flank shine as well-brushed horse-flesh shines. The zebra clatters its
hooves on the unsympathetic cobbles. The man encourages the zebra
into the zoo building. The wind rustles in the trees.*

65. ALBA'S APARTMENT
ALBA *sits up with a start in her bed – a bed lit with patches of light
and dark from the street lights. She strains to listen. There are sounds
from the zoo, the sounds of an animal in pain. She makes a natural
movement towards the window, but is pulled up short by her crippled
condition. She listens in the dark, her mouth open and dry.*

66. AT THE TIGER CAGE
Early morning. OLIVER *has shut himself in the tiger cage. The same
cage where the pacing tiger has worn away the paintwork. A small
crowd has gathered in front of the cage.* FALLAST, PLATE, PIPE,
VAN HOYTEN *and a number of press photographers and others.*
OLIVER *in the cage, nervously walks up and down.* OSWALD *and*
DE MILO *are on the other side of the cage, near the cage service
door.* OSWALD *talks to his brother through the bars in the most
offhand way he can muster, helping to keep up his brother's, and his
own courage. The tiger pays little attention to the commotion. With
feet splayed, it concentrates on eating a hunk of yellowing meat,
probably the head of a zebra.*
OSWALD: Come on Oliver, you've done enough.
OLIVER: Enough? This tiger walks ten miles up and down this
cage every day.

MILO: Do you really think it'll walk fewer miles with you inside
   him . . . in a striped flannel suit with a pen in the top
   pocket and a crease in the trousers?
OLIVER: (*Smiling bravely*) Maybe I should take a few clothes off
   to make it easier.
MILO: You're supposed to let the animals out, not go in there
   with them.
OLIVER: How can I let out a tiger? They'd only shoot it.
FALLAST: (*Shouting*) Oliver, if you don't come out, we'll shoot
   it anyway, which will not, I would have thought, have
   served your dubious purpose.
OLIVER: What would suit your purpose, Fallast? An export
   business in tiger skins? There's not enough room in this
   bloody cage even for a striptease. (*Struggling to get out of his
   trousers.*)
PLATE: What have you got that's so big, Oliver?
   (*There is dirty laughter from the pressmen.*)
OSWALD: (*Suddenly making a decision and taking off his jacket*)
   Look, I think I'd better join you.
MILO: Oswald! One fool in there is enough.
FALLAST: Stop him.
PLATE: It's a sympathy-strip.
VAN HOYTEN: Why don't you join them, Milo?
   (*There is dirty laughter from the crowd which moves forward to
   take pictures with flash-lights as* OSWALD *enters the cage.*)
FALLAST: What on earth are they trying to prove?
VAN HOYTEN: (*With heavy sarcasm*) Why, that they are
   brothers, of course.
   (MILO *screams and starts forward.*)

67. VAN MEEGEREN'S SURGERY
Two paintings by Vermeer hang high up on the wall of VAN
MEEGEREN's *white-painted studio. They hang symmetrically side
by side. They are of Vermeer's 'The Astrologer' and 'The
Geographer', two paintings of what could be the same man or
identical twins.*
*As the camera is fixed on the paintings, the sound track is a
continuation of the previous scene. Jostling, the clang of metal bars,*

then a snarl from the tiger; shouts from the crowd. The camera tilts or cranes down from the paintings to the two brothers sitting symmetrically on chairs in VAN MEEGEREN's *surgery.* VAN MEEGEREN *has his back to the camera. The brothers are naked for a medical examination. Superficial scratching from the tiger has marked their bodies symmetrically down the sides where they were joined as children: along the arms, the waist and the upper thigh. The scratching has been neatly bandaged in places, and there are a few medical stitches on both bodies just above the hip.*

VAN MEEGEREN: The tiger was obviously making a prophetic gesture? (*He laughs sarcastically.*) I can consider the possibilities of joining you together, but between us, could we satisfy the experts?

OLIVER: You seemed to have satisfied the experts before.

VAN MEEGEREN: Meaning?

OLIVER: By providing the zoo with a one-legged gorilla.

VAN MEEGEREN: Do you feel that the gorilla was ill-used?
(*The brothers look at one another.*)

VAN MEEGEREN: If you feel that my care is incomplete, I must look at the animal again.

OLIVER: What for, to amputate its other leg? If it's painful, cut it off. Is that your answer?

VAN MEEGEREN: (*With a smile*) Animals, on the whole, are designed with a view to symmetry. Surely in your experiments you must have noticed? One of decay's first characteristics is to spoil that symmetry, wouldn't you say?

OLIVER: You leave that animal alone, Meegeren.

VAN MEEGEREN: Dear me. What do you think I am?

OLIVER: You're certainly not Vermeer.

OSWALD: Was it really necessary to amputate a second time on Alba Bewick?

VAN MEEGEREN: Yes it was. (*Indignantly.*) And if you doubt my abilities I wonder why you are here?
(*The brothers are silent.*)

VAN MEEGEREN: Why do you want it done?

OLIVER: Completeness.

VAN MEEGEREN: (*After a pause*) I will do it for nothing. Though I understand that you are rich.

OSWALD: That is just not true.

VAN MEEGEREN: ... but you could (*insinuatingly*) help me.

OLIVER: How?

VAN MEEGEREN: I am Alba Bewick's surgeon – I have been Alba Bewick's adviser – I wish to be her friend ... and more than her friend ... you could help me a great deal. (*The brothers look at one another.*)

OLIVER: What do you want us to do?

VAN MEEGEREN: For a start ... let me be the father of her child.

OSWALD: (*With* OLIVER *echoing*) No! (*There is a silence*)

VAN MEEGEREN: I could help you maybe even more ... I notice, Oswald, that all your experimental subjects have been female ... Do you envisage taking your photographic experiment to completion? Milo is a good friend of mine. She weighs 126 pounds ... she is five foot six inches in her stocking-feet. One inch shorter than your wife, I believe ... like your wife ... she is now ten weeks pregnant. The child is mine ... she may very well have an abortion ... I can perform it. There could be complications ... and I can juggle the outcome ... (*The brothers stand up together in indignation. Their tiger wounds match symmetrically.*)

VAN MEEGEREN: You see how much I am prepared to bargain for? ... stand together ... you see, it could be made to work ... I could stitch you together ... for a price ... ?

68. ZOO LABORATORY – DOG DECAY
On OSWALD's *time-lapse film the heavily marked black and white Dalmatian dog decays in a black box marked with a white grid. Four weeks of decay is shortened into twenty seconds of time-lapse film.*

69. IN OSWALD'S APARTMENT
OLIVER *and* OSWALD *have been interrupted by* VAN HOYTEN *and* PLATE *in the act of trying on their 'double-suit'. It's unfinished, with the tacking, the French chalk and the pins still in evidence and*

the lining hanging out of the pockets. The suit material is noticeably black and white. Pinned on to the wall of the room are the paper patterns made for the suit by MILO. *Prominent on the newspaper patterns is the photo of the car crash. A television is switched on in a corner of the room showing the eighth programme in the series of 'Life on Earth' films – it is featuring monkeys.*

VAN HOYTEN: ... a pregnant zebra will cost you four hundred pounds.

OSWALD: Four hundred? It's zoo property, you can't ask that.

VAN HOYTEN: I have decided to forget the spotted dog ...

OSWALD: God, *you've* decided?

VAN HOYTEN: ... but you're certainly obliged to pay for this animal.

OLIVER: I want to know how it died.

PLATE: Neither of you were that curious about the swan or the crocodile ... (*He sniggers.*) ... and if you can afford one of Milo's black and white suits, you can afford a zebra.

VAN HOYTEN: ... and now that the photographic experiments are approaching a climax ... (*Nodding at the TV.*)

OSWALD: What do you mean?

VAN HOYTEN: Evolution as *you* know it, Oswald, undoubtedly, and for the moment, ends with man ... some say woman.

PLATE: ... and an apple.

VAN HOYTEN: How do you anticipate completing your enquiry? ... how much would you pay, do you think, for a human corpse?

OSWALD: (*Smiling*) God, Hoyten, I really believe you mean it.

VAN HOYTEN: Milo is about your wife's build and age and weight and she's pregnant ... with my child.
(OLIVER *and* OSWALD *laugh out loud.*)

VAN HOYTEN: So what's amusing you?

OLIVER: That Venus de Milo is unusually fertile or rather careless ...

OSWALD: For someone without arms.

PLATE: Arms?

OLIVER: It doesn't matter.

VAN HOYTEN: A little persuasion and I know that Milo is ready to visit the zebras ... zebras are notoriously fickle, very

possessive with their mares . . . especially Grevy's Zebra.
You know, the one with the soft eyes and the sharp hooves
and the vicious kick?

PLATE: . . . and the big prick?

OSWALD: You deceive yourself, Hoyten . . . just to thwart you
alone I'd make sure Milo never died . . . here's £400 for one
female Grevy's Zebra . . . killed no doubt in a corner, but
for the same four hundred, you must put in the
tranquillizer-gun.

VAN HOYTEN: (*Smiling*) Good Lord, you aren't thinking of
doing your own killing, are you? I advise against it. You're
an amateur.

70. ALBA'S ZOO HOTEL APARTMENT BEDROOM
ALBA, *very pregnant, sits up in bed. The room is full of yellow
flowers.*

OLIVER: Milo has found you Felipe Arc-en-Ciel.

ALBA: You're kidding. He'll be just in time. (*Holding her belly.*)

MILO: He's waiting in the lift.

ALBA: (*Intrigued*) What's he doing there?

OLIVER: Oh, he's making adjustments so that he can meet you
on an equal footing.

ALBA: I'm nervous.

MILO: You needn't be. He's handsome, reserved and
surprisingly sanguine.

ALBA: How – how did it happen for him?

MILO: Fell off a horse.

ALBA: A horse? Is he rich?

OLIVER: Do you have to be rich to own a horse?

ALBA: Are there many horses left?

MILO: Enough to see them through, which is maybe more than
you can say for zebras.
(*The door is pushed open and* OSWALD *wheels in*
ARC-EN-CIEL.)

ALBA: (*Whispered aside to* OLIVER) I thought you said he had
legs?

OLIVER: He's taken them off to meet you.

FELIPE: Hello. Felipe Arc-en-Ciel. (*Indicating himself.*)

99

ALBA: Hello. (*Smiles all round and a pause, brashly filled by* ALBA.) I am a whore for freaks – separated Siamese twins a speciality.

FELIPE: I have been told, madam, of your enjoyments. I sympathize. I, madam, an an inordinate admirer of horses – pregnant mares especially – I've always wished that I could have serviced a white pregnant mare . . .

MILO: And have you tried?

FELIPE: . . . in this present maimed company I can admit to anything. A white mare was my downfall – literally. I was tossed and kicked . . . but I still lust . . . after riding her. Her name was Hortensia. (*The company laughs, including* FELIPE.)

ALBA: I am jealous already, for has not a horse *four* legs?

FELIPE: Then that, madam, is just enough for both of us. (*He kisses her.* MILO *watches him with great interest.*) . . . and this, Milo, is for you, for bringing us together. (*He hands her a magazine where 'The Obscene Animals Enclosure',* MILO's *story, has been published.*) My other alias is Mr Ted Chimera . . . (*They all laugh.*)

71. GORILLA HOUSE
At night in the rain.
Outside the gorilla/ape house at the zoo, the Deuce twins with the help of MILO *break into the Ape House.*
Leaving MILO *smoking a cigarette and keeping watch on the porch, the brothers, in the near pitch-darkness, search for the correct cage with a torchlight. Grumblings and mutterings come from the dark cages. They move along a succession of caged animals until they come to the cage of the one-legged gorilla.* OLIVER *loads the dart-gun and pokes it between the bars.*
Outside, MILO *winces at the faint sound of the 'mercy' pistol.*

72. ZOO LABORATORY
The Deuce brothers have arranged the gorilla on to the photographic bed of the time-lapse camera. OSWALD *has taken the 'scientific' aspects a little further – the gorilla is tagged with red and blue ribbons. The door of the laboratory opens and in comes* FALLAST,

PLATE, VAN HOYTEN, VAN MEEGEREN, BOLNES *and* PIPE.
FALLAST *and* BOLNES *carry handkerchiefs to their faces.*
FALLAST: What makes you two think you can behave so
cavalierly in this zoo?
OSWALD: We have saved this animal from further mutilation.
VAN MEEGEREN: By killing it?
OSWALD: Thanks to you it was ailing and has been for three
years. (*He produces the photos of the gorilla taken at the start
of the film.*)
VAN MEEGEREN: Is that for you to decide? (BOLNES *tears up the
photos.*)
OLIVER: This zoo is run by incompetents and mountebanks.
VAN HOYTEN: I wonder why you've stayed here so long?
FALLAST: But you needn't stay any longer. You're fired.
OSWALD: On what excuse?
FALLAST: Maltreatment of animals for one . . . misuse of zoo
property for another . . . unauthorized freeing of
animals . . .
OSWALD: We haven't finished.
FALLAST: Finished what? Some bogus experiment that satisfied
your obsessional grief. What valuable conclusion can be
gained from all this rotting meat? Nothing. How can you
measure decay?
OLIVER: By degrees of grief perhaps?
OSWALD: (*Looking at* VAN HOYTEN) Or by planning a zoo
devoted to black and white animals because you're colour-
blind . . .
OLIVER: . . . and making sure there's no opposition by killing
off all the black and white animals that aren't yours?
OSWALD: By using a zoo for some exotic game of barter and
blackmail?
OLIVER: (*Looking at* VAN MEEGEREN) . . . or by maiming
animals so that they can be expensively patched up?
(JOSHUA PLATE *hurls himself on* OSWALD. *A fierce fight is
heard on the soundtrack.*)

73. ALBA'S APARTMENT
Two naked, newly delivered boy twins lie on white sheets beside the

white, sweating, exhausted ALBA. *The Deuce brothers enter, cut, bruised, bleeding. At once, great delight and surprise register on the brothers' faces.*

OSWALD: Good grief, Alba, you kept that quiet.

OLIVER: How did you manage one each?

ALBA: I thought I had failed. After all they are not Siamese.
(*Each brother picks up a child.*)

ALBA: Careful! So where were you?

OSWALD: We were busy. How did you do it?

ALBA: I just sat on the eggs. What do you mean you were busy?

OLIVER: What are you going to call them?

ALBA: Castor and Polydeuces?

OSWALD: . . . from the rape of the swan?

OLIVER: Too obvious.

ALBA: Gamma and Delta?

OLIVER: Wrong sex.

ALBA: Do Greek letters have a sex? And what's the excuse for the bruises?

OSWALD: It's not important. Did you know?

OLIVER: You must have known?

ALBA: No, I can safely say I didn't know, but I should have guessed. And what's not important?

OLIVER: We've been fired, sacked, dismissed, thrown out . . .

ALBA: From the zoo? . . . What was the last straw? Did you photograph a camel with a broken back?

OLIVER: How are you?

ALBA: Tired and my feet itch. So does my back.

OSWALD: Who was here?

ALBA: A midwife and the hotel porter and Felipe and Milo.

OLIVER: I'm sorry we weren't here.

ALBA: So am I.

OSWALD: Are you pleased?

ALBA: Of course. Now give them back. (*The twins put the children back on the bed.*) What are you going to do now?

OSWALD: Continue.

ALBA: Where and with what?

OLIVER: We thought you wouldn't mind us working at L'Escargot.

74. L'ESCARGOT
Night time at L'Escargot. The brothers cut and saw wood planks to build a platform/scaffold in the centre of the rich, lush garden at L'Escargot.

BETA *has collected jars of butterflies, insects, newts, spiders, and is in the act of sticking on labels – simple names like 'Brown Insects'/'White Bugs'/'Green Grubs'/'Red Ones'/'Yellow Ones'.*

OLIVER: What are you doing?

BETA: Making a zoo.

OLIVER: Can I look?

BETA: If you pay. (*She has a box reserved for money.*)

OSWALD: The old story.

OLIVER: But with a brand new taxonomy. Only an innocent would put a spider and a fly in the same cage because they were both brown.

OSWALD: Putting them together will probably tell an innocent more about spiders and flies than keeping them apart.

BETA: And you mustn't cheat.

OLIVER: Cheat?

BETA: I must mark the back of your hand with ink (*She flourishes a pen*) to make sure you've paid.

OSWALD: Whatever for?

BETA: Now you look so alike, I can't tell the difference between you any more.

75. IN THE ZOO HOTEL APARTMENT
ALBA *lies in bed. She looks worn and exhausted but still attractive, her red hair spread out on the pillow.*

OSWALD: We've got L'Escargot ready. When will you be allowed to come?

ALBA: I'm well enough, but I'm not coming.

OLIVER: (*Very surprised*) Why ever not?

ALBA: I'm ill. Van Meegeren says my spine is damaged.

OSWALD: God, why listen to him? Haven't you had enough of him?

ALBA: I'm not coming. I want to stay here . . . near the hospital . . . (*Said with a smile*) near the zoo. (*After a pause.*) But I am well enough to tell you something that I know you're not going to like. (*After another pause.*) I do not want you to be the legal father of my children.

OLIVER: You what . . . ?

OSWALD: Van Meegeren has squeezed that out of you.

ALBA: Good Lord no. I want you to . . .

OSWALD: (*Adamantly*) We are the father. (*They look confused at the problems of grammar.*)

ALBA: (*With a smile*) You see?

OLIVER: Bad grammar doesn't signify anything.

ALBA: 'They went in in twos and they came out in twos'. It's stopped raining. (*She looks towards the window.*) I've found my Arc-en-Ciel. (*Both brothers make a cursory glance towards the window.*) I cannot have my children having three parents.

OSWALD: God, what difference does that make?

ALBA: The children can only have one father.

OLIVER: We are the father.

OSWALD: We are their natural father.

ALBA: Felipe will be their father.

OLIVER: Never.

ALBA: Listen. You found Felipe for me, you and Milo. He's an ideal father. Grief has made you unreliable. On your own admission, you are jobless. I cannot risk your extreme behaviour.

OSWALD: You risked it before.

ALBA: It's too much responsibility for you . . . and you would be prevented from being together.

OSWALD: Nonsense.

ALBA: Felipe will make a better father.

OLIVER: He's legless.

ALBA: Did that stop me being a mother?

OSWALD: Motherhood is involuntary.

ALBA: Now what percentage of lays are interested tries at fatherhood?

OSWALD: We'll take legal advice.

ALBA: Oswald, stop being petulant and what would you gain? I'm sure that unmarried male twins don't make a good legal

precedent. Beta now can't even tell which of you is which. In a courtroom I can't imagine that you would win, and if you did, you would know it was against my wishes.
(OLIVER *turns to the window and puts his fist through the pane. It shatters.*)

76. L'ESCARGOT — THE ZEBRA DECAY

The footage of the decaying zebra fills the screen. The most ambitious of the decay projects, filmed over a period of weeks, the film occupies two or three minutes. The zebra decays slowly. The film is being projected in the open air on the platform built by the Deuce brothers at L'Escargot. Moths and insects whirr and hum in the projector beam, the garden is spectrally lit by arc lamps. There is the sound of cicadas and a distant nightingale. There are distant lights from the house that goes with the garden which is some six hundred yards away behind lighted thick-leafed trees. A lighted lamp hangs in the centre of the platform built by the twins, visited by more moths and other insects. It swings gently in a breeze. Seated watching the film are the twins. They are seated close together wearing dark suits. BETA's *zoo, having proliferated with more jam jars, bottles, tin trays and basins, is spread out around them, with* BETA *asleep in a deck-chair, partly covered by a blanket. The twins comtemplate the screen.*

OLIVER: Do you think Adam was a Siamese twin?
OSWALD: What happened to his brother?
   (*The twins get up in perfect unison, as one movement, It is realized that they are wearing the suit made for them by Milo. Wide shot of the brothers standing on their platform in the middle of the lit garden. They are both illuminated and silhouetted by the light beam from the projector.*)

77. ALBA'S ZOO HOTEL APARTMENT

Evening, the last light coming in through the window. A colour TV screen showing the last programme in the series of 'Life on Earth' — the programme that shows the evolution of man. The images are beautiful — of primitive naked tribesmen and women.

ALBA: (*Sitting up in bed*) . . . all that way (*Indicating TV*) to bring me to this. (*Briskly*.) Now, I want you to be here tonight – and I mean it – no prior engagements. Bring Beta's record and you can watch me go.

OLIVER: Go? Where are you going?

ALBA: (*Cheerfully*) I've had enough.

OSWALD: What do you mean?

ALBA: (*Briskly*) My children are now spoken for . . . aren't they? (*When there is no reply*.) . . . aren't they? (*The twins nod*.) . . . and I'm exhausted. The swan succeeded in the end.

OLIVER: I'm busy tonight, so you can't go tonight.

ALBA: Oh? What are you doing that's so important?

OLIVER: I'm grieving.

ALBA: Still?

OLIVER: Always. I'm now childless as well as wifeless.

ALBA: You've forgotten jobless and homeless.

OSWALD: We'll strike a bargain.

ALBA: God, thanks for thirty seconds of your sympathy. No bargains.

OLIVER: No record.

ALBA: No record? (*Incredulously*.) I'm not going to bargain over a gramophone record. You can stay away.

OSWALD: We'll come . . . on one condition.

ALBA: (*Laughing*) Don't tell me, I know. You want my corpse. God! My body for a gramophone record and a visit from a pair of Siamese twins. Haven't you had enough of my body?

OLIVER: You're our last chance.

OSWALD: And you were my first choice.

ALBA: Well, thank you both.

OSWALD: . . . and we need the use of the garden at L'Escargot . . . for nine months . . .

ALBA: A significant period.

OLIVER: . . . or longer.

OSWALD: We feel we can ask this because we have given up legal parenthood.

ALBA: (*Smiling*) You've learnt a thing or two from that zoo,

haven't you, even if it's only how to bargain. (*Laughing*.)
All right, all right . . . in the interests of science . . .
(*Disparagingly*) some science, you can have it, if you can get
it. But I know you won't get it because I now have a family
and you know what families are for . . . ?

OSWALD: With your permission in writing how can they stop us?

ALBA: Easily. They could try the words 'insanity' or
'insanitary'.

OLIVER: It has long been respectable to leave your body to
medical science.

ALBA: What's scientific about watching a body rot?

OSWALD: You always said you wanted to go back to L'Escargot.
So we'll take you.

OLIVER: And you can lie quietly in the garden . . .

ALBA: With you watching?

OSWALD: Only the camera will be watching.

ALBA: What's the point of watching *me*. My body's only half
here.

OLIVER: Then you'll fit better into the film frame.

ALBA: (*Laughing*) God, I should have known. Maybe you've
always been in league with Van Meegeren. A fine epitaph:
here lies a body cut down to fit the picture.

78. ZEBRA ENCLOSURE
The large blue letters of ZOO are illuminated from within. MILO,
*smoking a cigarette, paces up and down outside the bars of the zebra
pen . . . her shadow is long in the white lights from beside the zebra
house. She keeps looking towards the animals inside the enclosure,
whose shadowy forms are seen against the light, their breath
condensing on the night air. They occasionally snort and neigh.* VAN
HOYTEN *quietly approaches.*

VAN HOYTEN: Good evening, Milo. It's a clear night.

MILO: (*Dismissively*) It's not like you to speculate on the
weather.

VAN HOYTEN: Just the sort of night you've been waiting for
perhaps? Isn't it about time you decided to do what you've
been wanting to do for as long as I've known you, Milo?
(*He smiles.*)

MILO: (*She throws away her cigarette*) Have you got a flat piece
of plastic?
VAN HOYTEN: Yes. (*He hands it to her.*)
MILO: And a sharpened pencil?
VAN HOYTEN: Yes. (*He hands it to her.*)
MILO: You *are* well equipped.
VAN HOYTEN: Yes, I am.
(MILO *busies herself with the padlock. It opens, she takes off
her shoes.*)
MILO: Here, hold these for me. (*He does.*)
(MILO *goes through the gate and disappears in the darkness.
There is the sound of hooves and a vague cloud of dust drifts in
the light.* VAN HOYTEN *tosses the shoes over the wire, pauses
and then walks off. The dust settles.
There is the sound of zebras neighing, jostling, hooves, snorting
and female laughter and a scream and more laughter.*)

79. DEATH OF ALBA IN THE ZOO HOTEL APARTMENT
*In the zoo hotel suite at night. Low shaded lamps in the room,
around* ALBA'*s bed. A nurse in attendance, plumping pillows.*
OSWALD *sits on one side of the bed.* OLIVER *is at the open window
listening to the late night noises in the street: distant traffic, a far-off
radio, an animal cry at the zoo. The nurse leaves. There is a pause.*
OLIVER *leaves the window and comes and sits on the bed, the
opposite side to his brother.*
ALBA: Well . . . here we go. (*With a sigh.*) What's the time?
OSWALD: One o'clock.
ALBA: It won't be long . . . I didn't make the twenty-six
children of the alphabet.
OLIVER: You made an encouraging last fling.
ALBA: . . . besides (*Dismissively*) I can't think of too many
names that begin with Zed . . . I'm the last at L'Escargot.
From hereon, it's yours, along with my corpse . . . don't
worry, the papers are signed and sealed.
OSWALD: If you are the last, we are already finished.
ALBA: (*Smiling*) A Zed and two noughts. What a zoo. All right
(*Briskly*) . . . don't do anything with my body *I* wouldn't do

. . . now I want to lie still and quiet and put on Beta's record.

(OLIVER *puts* BETA's *record 'An Elephant Never Forgets' on the record player. It's only on for thirty seconds when* OSWALD *starts up.*)

OSWALD: God, she's gone. What are the signs?

OLIVER: No pulse (*he feels her wrist*) . . . no eye movement (*he lifts her eyelid*) . . . no breathing (*he puts his ear to her mouth*) . . . no heartbeat (*he feels her chest*) . . . the skin pales (*he looks at her face*) . . . and becomes stiff (*he takes her hand.*) . . .

OSWALD: Turn off that awful record.

OLIVER: Wait until it's finished.

(*Both brothers sit still, symmetrically, on either side of the bed. The record finishes.*)

OLIVER: Now what? (*They both sit stunned.*)

OSWALD: We take her to L'Escargot.

OLIVER: In a coffin?

OSWALD: For decency's sake, we take her in a coffin.

OLIVER: In a long or a short coffin?

OSWALD: I'm sure Alba would have been amused by a short coffin. At least it leaves no room for artificial legs.

(*There is a noise outside the door – of voices. The door opens and* FELIPE ARC-EN-CIEL *in a wheelchair,* BETA *and the nurse carrying the sleeping twins, enter.* BETA *crosses the room, kisses her mother, takes off the still spinning record from the turntable, and solemnly presents it to the brothers.*)

BETA: I can see that you're upset and you like animals, so I'll give you this as a present.

(BETA *then sits on* ARC-EN-CIEL's *lap in the wheelchair.*)

OLIVER: In a long or a short coffin? (*Nodding at the group by the door.*)

OSWALD: I don't think that it's going to be for us to decide. (*Speaking very resignedly.*) The family are here. I'm sure they'll want a long coffin. (FELIPE *quietly nods in agreement.*)

OLIVER: And we'll not be taking Alba to L'Escargot to film her decay? (FELIPE *nods quietly and understandingly in agreement.*)

109

OSWALD: (*After a pause, and looking at his brother.*) Well . . .

80. L'ESCARGOT

*A warm, mellow night in summer. The scaffolding built by the
Deuce brothers stands in the centre of a wild garden of greenery. The
wooden platform has a black floor, ruled off in six-inch squares by
thin white lines. The platform is roofed with wood and canvas, as is
the camera on its elaborate tripod. The camera is angled down on to
the black squared floor. Numerous electric cables and leads trail off
towards the house, which is lost in the greenery and long grass.
The Deuce brothers, clean, shaved, bathed and looking absolutely
identical with slicked-down hair and wearing their double-suit and
walking impeccably, come down the path across the grass. Without
ungainliness in their double-suit,* OLIVER *plugs the record player
into a spare socket among the tangled wires and puts on* BETA's
*record – the 'Teddy Bear's Picnic.' The brothers carefully undress,
hang the suit neatly on a hanger, make last adjustments to the
camera.
The brothers take hypodermics and inject themselves and lie down.*
OLIVER: God, this floor's hard.

    (*They touch at shoulder, thigh, calf and ankle. They die
quickly. The record finishes. One has his mouth open and his
eyes shut, the other has his eyes shut and his mouth open.
The snails come out in the failing light. They glide up the
camera tripod, crawl across the naked bodies, along the arm of
the record player which regularly lifts and falls, up the hanging
suit. The snail bodies glisten in the intermittent light-flash. A
snail crawls into* OLIVER's *mouth. The flashes come regularly
at the beats of the record music. A snail crawls around the lens
of the camera and across the electrical equipment, eventually
fusing the apparatus. The lights begin to flicker and stutter. As
dawn breaks, they finally go out. The final experiment
requiring the brothers' personal self-sacrifice comes to nought.*)